STILLBORN GALLERY

AXL BARNES

To Daniela,

Thank you for your support & friendship!

All the best,

Ax Barnes

Copyright © By Quill and Lantern Publishing 2021 and Axl Barnes 2021

Cover Art By: Thomas Stetson and Soluções Designe Arts - SD ARTS
@sdesignerarts

All Rights Reserved

By Quill and Lantern Publishing

First Edition

This is a work of fiction. Names, characters, business, events and incidents are the products of the author's imagination. Any resemblance to actual persons, living or dead, or actual events is purely coincidental.

Warning: the unauthorized reproduction or distribution of this copyrighted work is illegal. Criminal copyright infringement, including infringement without monetary gain, is investigated by the FBI and is punishable by up to 5 years in prison and a fine of $250,000. All rights reserved. No part of this book may be reproduced or transmitted in any form without written permission from the publisher, except by a reviewer who may quote brief passages for review purposes.

CONTENTS

Epigraphs	v
Introduction	vii
Numbskull	1
Closing Shift	15
Night Soil	23
The Playground with Crosses	35
Natasha Suicide	39
Florica, The Legend	45
A Perfect Day	51
Sunday Exit	57
Dead Seed	87
About Axl Barnes	133
About Thomas Stetson	135

"I long to be free—desperately free. Free as the stillborn are free."

    Emil Cioran, *The Trouble With Being Born*

"To step into death does not mean, as commonly believed, especially by Christians, to draw one's last breath and to pass into a region qualitatively different from life. It means, rather, to discover in the course of life the way toward death and to find in life's vital signs the immanent abyss of death."

    Emil Cioran, *On the Heights of Despair*

"External labor, labor in which man alienates himself, is a labor of self-sacrifice, of mortification."

    Karl Marx, *Economic and Philosophic Manuscripts of 1844*

"If we may assume as an experience admitting of no exception that everything living dies from causes within itself, and returns to the inorganic, we can only say *'The goal of all life is death'*, and, casting back, *'The inanimate was there before the animate.'*"

    Sigmund Freud, *Beyond the Pleasure Principle*

INTRODUCTION

Welcome to a grotesque universe where strangulation is the ultimate proof of love, youngsters morph into something less than zombies, happiness is but an invitation to suicide, and children beg to be smothered in their cribs. Mindless work provides no escape from this nightmare, as alienation can turn you into rotted produce or a blubbering mass of boneless flesh.

Stillborn Gallery collects nine nihilistic tales centered around the theme of mortality. Axl Barnes mercilessly uncovers the nest of maggots infesting the core of life. Each story comes with its own illustration by visionary artist Thomas Stetson, fitting together for a uniquely bleak and dazzling experience.

NUMBSKULL

With a murderous look, Ricky watched the new kid texting. Kids these days had no sense of responsibility, on the clock and still glued to their phones. Even more revolting, the spoiled brat sat on the chair at the desk in the cut fruit area, like he owned the place, headphones in his ears, head bobbing in the rhythm of some infernal music. Ricky made a mental note to talk to the store manager and make sure the kid didn't pass probation. He stormed through the stockroom's swinging doors and saw Brian out on the sales floor, working the wet rack. With his unusual gait—hunched back and tilted to the right—Ricky approached his older coworker.

"The new kid is beyond useless," Ricky barked.

Brian turned slowly and looked at Ricky with a mixture of pity and anxiety. The younger man was a bit too agitated for his taste. In Brian's view, Ricky, aka Rocky Balboa or The Rock, had been bullied as a kid and the extreme abuse jagged his brain into thinking he was a tough guy, an invincible hero. To those willing to listen to his bullshit, Ricky would brag that he never lost a fight despite his skinny build and small stature. Like Bruce Lee, he'd take on adversaries double his size and blindside them with his speed and the wrestling techniques he'd learned from decades of watching WWE—which he still believed was for real. Most co-workers felt sorry for him and, behind his back, they called him The Pebble, The Rock's younger and lesser-known brother.

Brian said, "What did you expect? Millennials...Good thing we're still here to keep this store afloat." He tossed a couple of mushy heads of lettuce into the garbage box on his cart.

"If it was up to me, I'd rip his head off and shit down his neck. I'd break his face and kick his teeth out," Ricky hissed.

"Well, it's a good thing it's not up to you then," Brian replied, tired of Ricky's outbursts and constant need for posturing.

With a nervous gesture, Ricky adjusted the bill of his Oilers cap. "So, how was your vacation?"

"Too short," Brian replied promptly. He had no clear recollection of it, like a forgotten dream. Only the store seemed real, the produce department.

"Did you hear what happened here? Did you watch the news?" Ricky asked.

"No, what happened?"

"Oh, my God, Brian, you *do* live under a rock. There was a fucking massacre here last Wednesday, murder-suicide, blood everywhere, the thing was all over the news!"

Brian bulged his normally sleepy eyes, his heart beating a tad faster.

"You remember Dylan from groceries?" Ricky continued. "He was in a relationship with Susan from deli, and then she dumped him for Kevin in pharmacy?"

Brian nodded despite the fact none of those names rang any bells.

"So, the cunt...not only did she dump poor Dylan, but she

started telling people that Kevin fucks her so much better than Dylan ever did. That Kevin showed her what sex is all about. And then guys started poking fun at Dylan, and he took a vacation. But he stopped by last Wednesday, carrying a butcher knife."

Brian's jaw dropped, his eyes ready to pop.

Ricky continued excitedly. "I was here in produce when I heard the shouts and the screams coming from pharmacy. When I got there, Dylan was on top of Kevin, stabbing him." Ricky made chopping motions with his right hand. "Blood flew everywhere. Susan jumped on Dylan to stop him, but he punched her away, got up, grabbed her hair, and slashed her throat. Then, he threw her on the floor and looked around wild-eyed. A crowd formed, but no one moved. I knew he was gonna run for the exit, so I ran ahead to block it and called 911. He ran down an aisle, heading for the doors. When he saw me, he stopped dead in his tracks. I took out my produce knife and said, 'Dylan, stop right there! The police are on their way. This is the end of the line for you buddy, you're trapped.' And you know what the crazy guy did?"

Brian shook his head, his jowls trembling.

"He cut his fucking throat, right then and there." Ricky ran his thumb across his neck and rolled his eyes up. "Some blood splashed my face and the till number one, and the floor. It was like in one of those Tarantino movies, *Kill Bill* or shit like that. I think he knew if he came at me, I would have killed him. We were friends, but that Dylan was gone. What I faced was a homicidal maniac. He knew better than to attack me, so he killed his sorry ass."

Brian knew Ricky might have embellished the story to make himself look good but didn't doubt the gist of it. "That's what they call a crime of passion if I'm not mistaken."

"Yeah, or Small Dick Syndrome," Ricky said and laughed, displaying his yellow horse teeth.

"Wow, I can't believe that happened in our store."

"Yes, the police were here and reporters, it was a fucking zoo. I was interviewed as a witness and was on the six o'clock news that day."

The Pebble's fifteen minutes of fame, Brian thought. He then prodded Ricky for more details, but his interest dwindled. He didn't seem to remember the people involved in this tragedy and couldn't imagine what consequences this disturbing event would have on his life. It was like watching the news, a story sparks one's curiosity, and then it's promptly forgotten once the sports segment comes on. As if it occurred in China or the dark side of the moon.

Ricky's attention was caught by a hooded woman carrying a red GoodLife gym bag and rushing toward the meat department.

"I think I know her. The low-life came to steal again," Ricky said through clenched teeth and trotted to the far corner of the produce area, a hunter chasing his prey. Brian knew The Pebble regarded himself as a Loss Prevention Officer and was always intent on catching thieves and hopefully beating them up or making them cry.

Brian turned his attention back to the wet rack to fill the green onions, cutting their ends neatly with scissors. He noticed the display stand for onions was almost empty, and his heart leaped with joy as filling up onions was the favorite part of his shift. That and doing some "sampling" of new products after the lunch break.

Brian was slowly getting into his groove when Ricky returned. "Did you see the God-awful Oilers last night? God, why they transfer Lucic Stone Hands is beyond me. Jesus Murphy...is he useless or what?"

Always down for talking hockey, Brian said, "Well, let me ask you this? Was Gretsky ever in a fight?"

Ricky lifted his cap, scratched his head, and frowned. He

didn't remember much about the Great One as he wasn't from Edmonton but grew up on the east coast. Back in those days, when puberty hit, all Ricky thought about was the Undertaker and the mystery of sex. "No?" he answered uncertainly.

"Well, of course not. Because he had his bodyguard, Dave Semenko. You always need a big body to protect your best player and scorer, which is McDavid now."

"But he's not scoring," Ricky whined.

"Well, that's because his line sucks, and I don't mean only Lucic. Let me ask you this, if they put their best players on McDavid's line, you think he's gonna have more points? Of course, he will. And the other lines just have one job: to keep the puck out of the net. Then we'll win every game cause the McDavid line will score each and every game."

Ricky didn't know what to make of Brian's theory and walked away, mumbling that the Oilers would miss the playoffs again. Back to his cart, Ricky began filling the banana stand.

Turning back to his work, Brian considered he never told Ricky that he rarely watched a game from beginning to end anymore. It was shameful, but it was part of his new outlook on life, his small secret about happiness. Brian would usually fall asleep after the first period of a hockey game. It was more the waiting for the game that pleased him, the fact the game was there, crowning his day, something to look forward to. It was some kind of ritual, him sitting on the couch, his dog sleeping on his feet and drooling on his slippers, the odorous shadow that was his wife yapping away on the phone in the kitchen, some fat singer belting out *O Canada*, the dimmed lights covering the room in a soft, warm amber glow. It was his end-of-the-day ritual.

Brian discovered the purpose of his life was sleeping. Like some people lived to eat, Brian lived to sleep. He liked to eat too, naturally, as he couldn't fall asleep on an empty stomach. The trick was to treat being awake as a means toward falling asleep. Exhausting himself, that was the key to happiness, so that the nightly sweet surrender to the care-free void of deep slumber would come without trouble. After more than forty years of working for the same grocery store, mostly in produce, Brian knew almost precisely the number of actions he needed to perform to get tired enough for his eight hours of bliss.

Around the time he turned fifty, Brian realized there was nothing to be gained in this world. His life was like a movie unfolding in front of him, more or less independent of his wills and wants—a boring old movie. Every day, same shit, different pile. He was like a lonely spectator in the private cinema of his mind, and the good thing about the cinema was it came with comfy seats in which he could snooze to his heart's desire. And no one kicked homunculus-Brian out of his cinema. After his revelation, Brian decided that he and his wife, lovingly nicknamed Saggy Naggy, should sleep in different rooms. Soon after, Brian discovered the joys of deep sleep, away from Saggy Naggy's farts, her incessant grinding of teeth, and lazy, slobbering blow-jobs. That had been by far the best decision of his life.

Brian guessed everyone knew, deep down, life was all about sleep. They were too arrogant to accept the simple truth. Ricky, for instance, got into fights hoping to get knocked out or put out of his misery. In his mind, the half-wit thought he was a hero, but all he craved was to be nothing, a hero wanting to be zero. This was the same with sex and drugs. The post-coitus sleep was the sweetest, and overdoses were exceedingly attractive because they offered sleep *and* the tantalizing chance of never waking up.

While philosophizing on the miracle of sleep, Brian continued working the wet rack with expert hands: celery bunches, celery sticks, cauliflower, radishes, broccoli bunches and crowns, green, yellow, and red bell peppers, and carrots. Culling and rotating, trimming and throwing away the wilted, spoiled veggies, cutting away the brown stuff. Making sure everything looked fresh and colorful. The rack underneath the vegetables was black, and the rule was no black ought to be visible. No holes. The customer's eye had to be attracted by a wall of vibrant colors.

Brian went through the same motions for nearly four decades. At sixteen his dad had thrown him out of the house for smoking pot and sleeping with 'girlfriends' who came too often and too loud. *A lifetime ago*, Brian mused. It felt like those things happened to someone else. Lately, it seemed to Brian, even his present life appeared to be someone else's. He felt no responsibility for his actions and no intimate connection to them. His life was like working the wet rack, pure habit.

The saying went, idle hands are the devil's hands. His hands never belonged to the devil, of that he was certain. But who did they belong to then? For a very long time, Brian would have proclaimed *his* hands were *his own*. But in the new reality-is-but-a-boring-movie world, doubt seeped into the foundation of that proclamation. Those weren't his hands but some hands belonging to God or his boss. He didn't care which. He only cared that if those hands stayed busy, he would get tired, sleepy.

Once he finished the rack, Brian went on his lunch break. Ricky's cart wasn't fully worked, two full boxes of bananas still waiting to be put away. *The numbskull complained about the new kid, but he wasn't doing much work either*, Brian thought with a pang of annoyance. He figured Ricky was off telling his heroic story to his crush in the deli or kissing the ass of some manager.

During his break, Brian ate the pizza and chicken wings

leftover from last night and read the sports section. The lunchroom was empty. The clock showed six pm but Brian wasn't sure exactly what day it was. Strangely, he felt he never left the store and that the clock was broken, crushed by its uselessness. What's more, suddenly, Brian realized he couldn't even *imagine* leaving work. What door would he use? How would the door open? Push? Pull? What would he do next? Feeling out of sorts, Brian went back to produce. He wanted a treat and remembered the bin full of watermelon they received. He decided to "sample" one with Ricky.

The younger man was still not in sight. Brian figured he'd show up sooner or later. He entered the stockroom, picked a watermelon, knocked on it to make sure it was ripe, peeled off its label, and set it on a table in the cut fruit area. The new kid was already gone, good riddance. Brian grabbed a big knife and cut the melon down the middle. Under the rind, the blade hit something hard. Puzzled, Brian cut sideways. What the gash revealed made him lurch. Under the watermelon's green skin, there was a layer of yellow skin and bone. His knife slashed into flesh, oozing rusty blood. The blood reeked.

Despite himself, he continued to cut the watermelon skin like an archeologist, carefully unearthing an ancient artifact. Soon there was no doubt, a human head was buried inside the fruit. He pressed on the eye socket, and his finger went through. A violent stench of excrement assaulted his nostrils, and he puked in his mouth, bits of barbecue chicken wings imbibed in bile. He swallowed back with a grimace.

How can this be? Brian's mind reeled, struggling to find purchase. Could a murderer grow a watermelon around a human head to hide it? Was the farmer who sold this some sort of serial killer? Were the other watermelons in the bin filled with other human body parts? A fruit naturally growing like that would violate a law of nature, surely. Breaking his stream of thought, buzzing flies came out of the hole, and Brian recoiled in disgust, letting go of the skull. For a brief moment, he thought the spoiled melon would roll over and spill its fetid content on the white, spotless table. It remained in a vertical position, however, starring at him through its empty socket like an ancient totem.

In a dazed rush, Brian opened a plastic bag, tossed the head and the watermelon peels inside, and dumped the bag in the big garbage bin. Then he washed his hands, put new plastic gloves on, filled his cart with twenty-five-pound bags of onions, and went out on the floor. However, even the ritual of peeling onions couldn't eclipse the troubling images in his head. As he touched every onion, he imagined a small skull inside it. Could it be newborn heads? The heads of pets? Or shrunk heads?

He remembered members of some ancient tribes would shrink the heads of their enemies to stave off revenge. Maybe the softer onions covered the still-forming skulls of fetuses? Maybe the moldy ones were the stillborn ones? As the thought occurred, his fingers pierced through a rotted bulb. He opened the bag and saw a gray gelatinous onion with white spots on it. At first, he thought it was mold or, more implausibly, bits of rice. But then he noticed the bits squirming and realized they were maggots. And next to the spoiled onion, there was a set of dentures. They looked a lot like Saggy Nagy's. Brian was also vaguely reminded of the Cheshire cat, except these dentures were grinning and grinding on dry, rusty onion leaves.

As fast as he could, Brian took the cart in the back and tossed the bag of onions away in the large garbage bin, on top of the melon skull. He freaked out. His heart thundered in his chest, palms sweated, mind fogged from anxiety. He needed Ricky, he needed to hear his stupid stories, he needed to talk to him about hockey—anything to forget the uncanny visions. He craved normalcy, weirdness made him anxious. How could he sleep when anxious? Brian peered down each aisle—coffee and tea, snacks and pop, pet food, frozen foods—but Ricky was nowhere.

The whole store was deserted and eerily quiet.

Brian figured he mistakenly stayed past closing time. He frowned and tried to think back on his actions. Abruptly, all the lights dimmed, amplifying his confusion. He turned in place, looking for someone, anyone, to ask for clarification. "Hello," he shouted with an unsteady voice. "Ricky, where the hell are you?" No answer.

There were no cashiers, no courtesy clerks, no customers. Through the murky light, he saw the two glowing exit signs on top of the automatic doors and an ad with the price of unleaded gas at the station next door. Outside, the lamps cast a pale glow over the empty parking lot. At this late hour of the night, no doubt the doors were closed.

Out of ideas, he was a puppet with its strings cut off. He stood at the entrance to the bakery area for a good five minutes, three hundred pounds of meat devoid of purpose. Slowly, his anxiety dissipated, the dimmed lights sedating his system. He imagined he was in the living room waiting for the angel of sleep. There was some weird, upsetting horror movie on TV, but he was getting tired, and that was all that mattered. The reassuring fantasy took hold as the store *was* a familiar place, kinda like home; it was *his* place.

He decided to look for Ricky in the stockroom. He walked there on leaden legs, the thickening grayness around him heavier and heavier. Ricky's cart was no longer on the floor, and the banana table was now full. *The idiot must be in the back.* Brian opened the doors and saw Ricky by the shelves full of banana boxes. Mr. Rocky Balboa slept on the bottom side of the cart, in a fetal position, his head on a five-pound bag of potatoes. *But how is this possible?* Brian asked himself. Ricky was short but was he that short?

Brian approached the cart and crouched down for a closer inspection. His knees popped loudly. It looked like it was only Ricky's clothes carefully arranged at the bottom of the cart to look like a human body. This reminded Brian of a documentary about the infamous escapees from Alcatraz. They tricked their guards by leaving behind dummies in their beds to cover their break-out. For a brief second, he thought he was maybe the butt of a practical joke and looked around, an embarrassed smile on his face. But everything was still; no one laughed at him.

Brian turned his attention to Ricky's clothes: scuffed-up black shoes, black jeans (although the company policy required dress pants), a gray shirt, and a green apron with the name tag. Brian lifted the Oilers cap. Underneath, there was a large, wrinkled potato with a dusty, rough texture. Five white sprouts came out of the tuber, four of them looking like a fetus's tiny limbs. On what appeared to be a bulbous head, the left eye was gone, and the right one looked like a small bag of puss. The nose was sucked inside. Only a couple of teeth remained. The fifth wormy sprout ran from the top of the fetus' head to the bag of Russets like an atrophied umbilical cord. Except the bag seemed to suck the nutrients out of the fetus-like potato, small globs of matter passing from the decaying vegetable into the bag.

A sound came from Ricky's remains—a low voice under a layer of radio static noise. Brian lowered and tilted his head so his good, left ear could decipher the words: "I took out...my produce knife and said 'Dylan, stop right there! The police are on their way. This is the end of the line for you buddy, you're trapped.... I'll cut you up, man! I'll cut you up you, scum...closed casket funeral when I'm done with you, you psycho'."

Brian covered his metamorphosed co-worker with the Oilers hat and stood. He wasn't shocked by the horrific visage. His exhaustion covered him like a cloak, his eyelids were heavy, and everything was too distant and insignificant. The real world was at the other end of the tunnel, a mess that had nothing to do with him, a boat that had left the shore. Nothing could disturb him now. His brain was numb, tired of processing a frustratingly chaotic world. Inside that numb-skull, homunculus-Brian was almost asleep in his private theatre. With zombie-like slowness, Brian grabbed a piece of cardboard, set it on the top side of the cart, and used a bag of potatoes for a pillow. He'd bunk with Ricky tonight as he'd bunked with his brother when they were kids. His heavy lids closed, and he was immediately transported into an underground world of rest and blessed, fertile rot.

CLOSING SHIFT

It was always the last hour that was the longest, time passing slower and slower. No customers, just the wait and aimless wandering. No more thoughts. I was reduced to being there, a body, defending the merchandise—shoes and menswear—from an unlikely thief. I couldn't do much in the last hour except fight a losing battle against boredom. Mandip, the woman in menswear, was folding until the last minute, like a machine, as if in some sort of trance, pushing her clothes folding table around like a walker. She wasn't ugly but suffered from some kind of chronic stomach pain and always looked on the verge of crying, dark circles under her eyes.

Once, Thomas, my schooled friend, explained to me Zeno's paradox. How you couldn't get from point A to point B because you had to cross half the distance first and then half of the remaining distance and then half of that and so on for all fucking eternity. That was how time felt in that last hour. As if every passing moment increased the gaping void ahead. The finish line became ever more distant, impossible to reach as if you were caught in a nightmarish race through quicksand.

In the background, Cher started singing: "Do you believe in life after love?/ I can feel something inside me say/ I really don't think you're strong enough."

Is there life after work? I asked myself. *Do you believe in life after rape?*

I was definitely not feeling strong enough. Thomas couldn't hang out after my shift, spending time with his stupid new girlfriend as usual of late. I told him he should share her, just for kicks, but he ignored me. Maybe he caught feelings for the cunt. When she wasn't around, we'd mostly get high and play first-person shooters, sometimes drug my mom's cat for fun. Of course, I could do all those things by myself, but it wouldn't be the same. I considered stopping at Safeway after work to buy junk food, but that desire wasn't strong enough either. I was there, enduring that final hour, with no hope or want to move me, just existing, breathing, aging.

My feet took me to the menswear area in a half-assed attempt to check out the new clothes, although most of them were too tight for me. They had cool shorts in the Point Zero brand, but they weren't on sale.

Suddenly, I noticed something on the floor by Mandip's folding table. I thought it was a pile of black clothes a customer had left behind, but a brown, organic mass stood on top of the pile. As I get closer, I recognized a face, Mandip's sad face. It appeared stretched and almost liquid. I gaped at her in shock. The whole thing seemed like one of those magic tricks where some bearded wizard brandishes a wand, and the monster disappears in a puff of smoke, leaving its clothes behind. Except, in this case, Mandip only half-disappeared. Her flesh remained, boneless, melted.

In the background, Cher's song gave way to Lady Gaga's *Born This Way*.

Mandip looked at me with crazed, pitiful eyes. They spread on her flattened face like sunny-side-up eggs with dark yolks. Her toothless mouth struggled to form words, "Jjjjjack, I don't ffffeel wwwwell..." She spoke with spittle flying from her crooked lips in a way that reminded me of Sylvester the Cat.

Tentatively, I took my cell phone out of my pocket and asked, "Should I call an ambulance?"

"No," she spat. "I have to shtay tillup the end of mmmy sshhift...jjjust a bit mmmmooore."

I stared in disbelief. "But...you seem to be dying."

"Noooo!! I'm ok, I'm sure I'll get bbbbetter later. I'm jjjust tired, you know? But I need to finish my sshhift for the mmmoney. I don't want my mmmanager to be mmmad at me and cut mmmy hoursh. Is ssshe hhere?"

Catherine, our manager, was also on the closing shift. She rarely ventured upstairs though. I looked around. "No sign of her," I reported.

"Good," Mandip mumbled and stayed there, waiting, her black, tearful eyes darting around to make sure no one saw her.

"Are you sure you're gonna be okay?" I probed.

"I'll be jjust fine," she said. "After I finish this sssshift and get home and make ssome tea. I'm jjjust exjausted. Worked sixsh days in a rrrrow."

I highly doubted some tea would fix Mandip's problem. I glanced down at her with pity and disgust. I didn't give a shit about her—not about anybody, except maybe Thomas. Sometimes I went through the motions to show I gave a fuck and was civil, but I wasn't. If all my coworkers died overnight, I wouldn't give a rat's ass.

Suddenly, with a flabby, trembling hand, Mandip lifted her

ID card toward me. "Will you help me sssswipe out ppplease...when ttttime comesh?" Obviously, she couldn't climb on top of the desk in her current state to swipe the card and punch in the required keys on the computer.

"Sure," I said. "I'll see you at closing time."

I hurried back to my department. On the plus side, the small incident killed time. My cell phone showed we only had half an hour left. I did a final walk through footwear to ensure no shoes were on the floor and no boxes on the display shelves and tables. I did the final clean-up at a snail's pace.

Soon, Catherine's voice came from the speakers. "Good evening customers, the store will be closing in fifteen minutes. Please take your final purchases to the nearest cash desk. The last doors open are on the main floor by the women's apparel department, at the Eastern exit."

Fifteen more minutes. Three times five minutes. Five minutes sounded more manageable. I pulled out my cell phone and browsed through pictures and vids of fresh meat on *Toiletwhores*. Ashley Sartre was almost as depraved as Tasha Suicide. Soon, the metallic sound of counting coins signaled the cashiers were closing the tills. I pocketed my phone and adjusted my boner. I went to the stockroom to grab my backpack with lunch leftovers, pop, and expired chocolate the store idiots wanted to throw away.

At five to nine, I headed to the cash register area to swipe out. Mandip was there, waiting patiently in between baskets full of clothes and other merchandise customers had returned throughout the day. She was grateful to see me. There were no more shoppers, and the cashiers focused on counting the money, paying us no mind.

I swept Mandip's ID card and pressed the required keys. Like a Jack-in-the-box, she stretched her rubbery neck to check the screen. The desired message popped up: *Well done! Thank you, and have a good day.* I returned her card, and she placed it in her purse. Then she slithered toward the escalator, like an octopus navigating the bottom of the sea, leaving a slimy track of blood and feces in her wake.

She used the escalator out of habit, without thinking, and my gut told me to stay behind and avoid any responsibility. I swiped out and waited. Mandip oozed down the metal steps. Sure enough, in a few seconds, screams pierced the quiet of the store. The cashiers and I ran to the top of the escalator.

As I predicted, the comb plate's metal teeth at the bottom of the stairs had pierced Mandip, shredding her clothes and amorphous flesh. The two cashiers stared in disbelief, their brains struggling to make sense of the gruesome sight. I didn't want to press the emergency stop. *Why ruin a perfect experience?* Mandip's flabby hands slapped against the metal platform, but she couldn't gain any purchase as her crumpled belly and tits and legs were ripped and chewed by the mechanism.

Blood and excrement splashed the metal steps and the glass of the balustrade as her agonized screams turned to blubbering and then a subdued gurgling. Gore and bits of flesh dripped in the pit below the stairs like meat from a grinder.

"Code white, code white!" Catherine screamed over the pager. "John, bring the first aid!" John was the guy from Loss Prevention. I saw Catherine run and press the emergency stop at the bottom of the stairs. Too little, too late for poor Mandip, who was a ripped, crumpled, stinking bag. I doubted a first aid kit would help. *Maybe call the cleaning lady,* I thought. *With a mop and a bucket.*

With the spectacle over, I made my way to the elevator and descended to the basement floor. On my way, I saw John run with his first-aid kit, and I bit down a smile. Talk about being useless. Through the employee exit, I stepped outside. The long summer day turned gray. I grabbed my smokes from the backpack and light one up. The nicotine struck my brain, and I had an idea. But it was too late, and the regret turned my legs to rubber.

I realize I played the whole thing wrong. I should have gagged Mandip, stuffed her in my backpack, and brought her home to play with. Maybe show her to Thomas the day after and see what he thought. Just for kicks.

NIGHT SOIL

Tanya forced herself to blow Kevin as he stood in cold silence. No "You're the best baby" or "That feels so good" came from him, no encouraging moans. Kevin's dick wasn't even fully hard, Tanya noticed distantly. This might take longer than she expected. She wouldn't have been surprised if she looked up to see him on his cell phone, possibly talking to another woman. Or maybe he was recording her giving head to make fun of with his friends later. She went harder, though her neck muscles were killing her. She caressed his balls and gently rubbed the erogenous area on top of his ass. Should she insert a finger in his butt or toss his salad? He usually lifted his legs and pressed down on her head if he wanted a rim-job. But he seemed aloof and disinterested, and there she was, trying to blow an expired hotdog.

Tanya chanced a glimpse up at Kevin. He looked at her like she was a purulent zit on his testicle, his lips pulled down in disgust.

"The Dick doesn't seem to like you anymore," Kevin said.

Tanya stood back and shrugged, partly relieved, partly

heartbroken, already tasting the bitterness of rejection underneath the fishy taste of pre-cum. "I made you come like twice last time. Am I doing something wrong?"

"No dear, it's not you. The Dick is just moody," Kevin said. "In fact, I'm not feeling so great myself. I'm coming down with something. I'm nauseated. I'll call it a night, but we should do this again soon." In a rush, Kevin got dressed and was at the door in record time. Tanya put her bra on, her panties, and her black skirt, trying to fight back the tears stinging behind her eyes.

"I'll call you next week, honey bun," Kevin said and kissed her on the cheek. He adjusted his black-rimmed glasses nervously, his sky-blue eyes avoiding hers. She'd loved those deep, penetrating eyes when they'd first met, and his roman nose and high and noble cheek-bones. Now she wanted nothing better than to punch that handsome face and hope the lenses would cut deep into those eyeballs. As if sensing Tanya's aggression, Kevin opened the door and stepped out in a hurry. The door banged behind him.

Tanya stared at the closed door, head lowered, shoulders slumped, a whirlwind of negative thoughts going through her mind. "Nauseated" meant Kevin found her gross. Did he have a better look at her stretch marks or belly fat? The wrinkles and veins on her boobs? Was her make-up running? "We should do this again soon" signaled he didn't want to see her again. "I'll call you" signified she shouldn't call *him*—as did the neutral kiss on the cheek.

Tanya collapsed on the couch. Did Kevin have another date lined up? Someone The Dick liked more? She chugged a beer to wash the taste of fuck-boy from her mouth. She burped loudly. What happened? Did she put on weight? Were her boobs too saggy? Something must have turned him off. He happily came in her month last weekend, no problem.

She sighed deeply. When would she learn not to mess

around with serial daters? They always acted nice initially—Kevin had brought her flowers on their first date—and ended up treating her like trash. Maybe they had a predatory sense, Tanya surmised, which signaled when the pray was insecure and had low self-esteem. Someone they could fuck and chuck, no strings attached, wham-bam-thank-you-ma'am.

A dark wave of dread and loneliness hit her. She looked at her cell phone on the coffee table, meaning to check if Kevin was available to chat on Facebook, but she couldn't make herself touch the phone. It appeared like a venomous snake. Surely, an avalanche of Tinder matches, direct messages, and dick pics awaited her. She looked away, hot tears brimming in her eyes and trickling down her cheeks. She wiped them away quickly.

You're not gonna cry after no fuck-boy. Tanya, get a hold of yourself!

She lay down on the couch, hugging a pillow to her chest and waiting for the thick shadow of depression to pass. That's when Andy started crying in the next room. Quickly, she stood up and rushed to check on her little boy. A wave of panic hit her when she turned on the light. He was puking black and oily vomit, the front of the Thomas the Train pajamas soiled. He sobbed. His face was red and twisted in agony. She ran to him and wiped his mouth with her hand. "What's that, baby?" she asked. It had the rich, musty smell of earth after rain. She frowned. Andy mostly had whole milk. How could he puke this dark substance?

Tanya got a clean towel from the closet and wiped Andy's mouth repeatedly till he stopped barfing. She changed the dirty pajamas with new ones, featuring dinosaurs, hugged and caressed him till his crying screams diminished. She changed the dirty pajamas with new ones, featuring dinosaurs. She ran to fetch her phone from the living room. In Andy's bedroom, she sat down on an easy chair by his crib, meaning to call an ambulance. Her thumb froze over the call button.

What if she was hallucinating?

She had been diagnosed with depressive schizophrenia in high school. Her hallucinations had always been primarily auditory. Except for one time when she had seen a large damp spot on the ceiling: spiders, black snakes, and roaches swarmed out of it. She fetched Andy and ran down to administration in a panic and alerted the maintenance guy. However, by the time he came up to her apartment, the ceiling looked absolutely normal, and he gave her an annoyed look that said: *How did you get out of the loony bin, young lady? And what genius let you take care of that poor baby? I wouldn't trust you to look after my cat.*

What if it was happening again? What if the doctors found nothing wrong with Andy and thought she just needed attention? Munchausen syndrome by proxy? She'd seen a chilling episode about it on *Forensic Files*. What if they decided she wasn't fit to be a mother and gave poor Andy to Matt, her ex? The thought was a cold fist squeezing her heart. She hated Matt. He didn't care for Andy. He was a narcissistic creep already abusing another hapless victim.

She pressed the buttons to call her mom instead, but a similar doubt crept into her mind, injecting paralyzing venom. Her mom wanted Andy to live with her. She'd insist Tanya resume therapy. Maybe she'd contact Matt, and together, they'd sign the papers to send Tanya to the loony bin.

"You suck," a tiny gargled voice said. The utterance was that of a child who sounded like he was choking and gasping for air. "You suck *asssss*." *Ass* was drawn out like the long hiss of a snake.

Tanya looked up from her phone, wide-eyed, mouth agape.

The voice came from Andy. His mouth wasn't moving to form the words, although he puked that damned black goo again. His eyes bore into her, tears replaced by pure hatred, his red face now pale, almost livid. "Why did you have me when you knew you were handicapped?" Heavy asthmatic breathing. "You made me into a handicapped too, you stupid cunt!"

Tanya looked at her son transfixed. The kid grabbed the edge of the pen with such force his tiny hands turned white. Then he shook the bars like a cage, his face stony, small teeth clenched in anger, round cheeks quivering slightly. His black eyes drilled holes into her.

Tanya felt something break deep in her psyche as if her meds stopped working all at once, and she fell through neural cobwebs into dark abyssal waters. Unable to bear Andy's stare, she covered her face and started crying. "I was just so lonely, I wanted someone to love, someone who won't reject me. I love you so much, baby! You're everything for me," she babbled. Deep down, she knew her gesture carried no weight. It was all for nothing and somehow far above her, in a sane world that rejected her, where every action was a futile exercise in nostalgia and resignation.

"Why didn't you get a dog, you dumb bitch?" the reply came, sharp as a scalpel. "I don't want to be your fucking pet. Why haven't you done humanity a favor and killed yourself once you found out you were an anomaly, a fucking abomination, a head case. Scum breeds scum, scab breeds scab. Fucked up people like you shouldn't procreate! You're just abusing the system, you crumb! Kill yourself and get it over with, but you'll have to kill me first. You have to the right the wrong."

Afraid of what she might do, of what her body might do, Tanya grabbed her phone and ran into the living room. Her ears buzzed like a radio frequency. She managed to send a short text to her mom.

Plz come over quick! I'm not well.

The whole apartment vibrated under the force of a dark magnetic field. Static noise boomed all around as if the walls suddenly turned into giant speakers. Andy's strangled baby voice came on again, from both inside and outside Tanya. "You can run, but you can't hide, you cumdumpster! I'm inside your body and mind. I'm part of you, unfortunately. I want to make this clear: I didn't want to be born, let alone be the companion of some deformed loser like you, a freak rejected by society. You forced me into this without my consent. My birth was a form of rape. How do you feel about that? You're into it, you fucking degenerate? Do you want me to just sit here and listen to you getting humped by a bunch of low-lives who don't have enough money for escorts? You want me to grow up without a father and other kids to pick on me for having so many 'uncles' and my mom being a broke slut? You have no right to do that. End it right now! I want no part of this!"

Tanya looked around in horror. This was her private apocalypse. The walls tremored like during an earthquake. Cans of beer and an ashtray on the coffee table fell to the floor. Paperbacks and knickknacks tumbled from the shelves. Through the torment of her inner cataclysm, Tanya saw the painful truth in her boy's judgment and understood his terrible command. It was true her life was a continuous torment with brief flashes of hope and joy that, in the long run, did nothing but amplify her suffering. She'd been living inside a prison, trapped behind the bars of dependency, paralyzed by insecurities. She was a mistake, an anomaly. She had no right to bring Andy into a hellish existence without his consent. What could she offer him? She was a mentally ill and clingy single mother living on government support—a pitiful vacuum of self-esteem.

Tanya sat in the hallway between the living room and Andy's bedroom, swaying under the gusts of dark thoughts like a lonely tree in a windswept field. She knew she had to end this. There was no light at the end of the tunnel. Hope was just a gateway for more suffering, a perverse invitation.

She went back into Andy's bedroom. The boy lay in his crib, his pillow covering his face. His tiny hand pressed on top of the pillow—that chubby hand weighing down on the pillow proved to Tanya all her hallucinations had a grain of truth to them. Her son was telepathically demanding to be killed.

She smothered him.

Sensing the approach to his final destination, Andy's tiny cold hand, a small, pink starfish, leached onto her own fingers and added its slight strength to the gruesome action. Tanya's last traces of sanity were erased when she heard Andy giggling under the pillow. As if she tickled him, sharing a happy moment, making a memory. His feet kicked, and she noticed he pissed himself. She knew it was from the overwhelming joy coursing through his tiny body, the cheerful anticipation of non-existence.

When Andy stopped kicking, Tanya dragged herself to the couch in the living room. The walls around her pulsed in the rhythm of her beating heart, relaxing and contracting. *It's as if the whole place is the womb of a woman in labor,* Tanya thought. And then she imagined a crack forming on the outside wall of her apartment, all the way up on the eleventh floor of the massive gray tower. A crack that became larger and larger, sending spidery zigzags throughout the cement. From within that crack, the labia of a vulva opened like pink butterfly wings. A jet of urine flew from the hole like pus from a throbbing zit. Thick blood oozed out, darkening the wall.

As if from the bottom of a water slide, two pink legs appeared first and then the whole baby dropped a few feet, as far as the electrical wires hung around its neck allowed. Tanya imagined neighbors coming out on their balconies to witness the miraculous birth. God gave them water from stone, and now a newborn baby came out of it as well. A baby that just hung there, like a tumor on the surface of a lung. The placenta came out next, a crumpled Dollarama bag, fetched by the wind. Tanya knew the hanging humanoid thing was just a plastic doll stuffed with garbage: insect and mouse traps, dust bunnies, used diapers and tampons, useless nuts and bolts. In her mind's eye, Tanya could see one of the doll's eyes was missing, roaches coming in and out, some copulating right there on its bald head.

"It's a boy," one of the women screamed with joy, noticing the penis that was in fact one of the rusty blades of a pair of scissors.

"Praised the Lord!" a man replied, raising his hands toward the leaden sky.

"Hallelujah!" another voice joined the chorus.

"It's a boy," Tanya mumbled to herself and screamed with hysterical laughter, tears streaming down her cheeks. "It's a boy! A baby boy! A garbage doll" she spoke louder, rocking back and forth on the couch, playing with a strand of her black hair, putting it in her mouth, and chewing on it.

Overwhelmed by terminal self-loathing, Tanya's crumbling mind turned toward self-mutilation. Except this time, it wasn't going be a timid cry for help like before—minor scratches with a razor over her wrists or superficial cuts on the rolls of fat padding her abdomen. No, none of that half-hearted stuff! Now, she needed to set things right for good and end this absurd struggle. Tanya decided her self-erasure should start with her genitals, the organs that gave her the most trouble, the source of all hope and misery. She remembered vaguely Dante's idea: those damned to Hell should give up all hope. The Italian poet got it all wrong. Hopelessness was the mark of Paradise. How can one be at peace if one still hopes?

Tanya grabbed a pair of scissors from one of the kitchen drawers, pulled down her skirt and panties, flopped back on the couch, and raised and spread her feet as if for a gynecologist exam. She rubbed her clit for a few seconds and then pulled it up, snipped it with the scissors, and flicked it on the floor. Then she pressed the tip of the top blade against her pussy and the bottom against her anus. She took a big gulp of vodka. She squeezed her eyes shut and stabbed. The blades punched through the two orifices easily, but no jolt of pain has rocked her body. It was as if she were under a heavy anesthetic. Tanya pressed down hard on the handles of the scissors, cutting the perineum muscle with ease. She expected warm blood to gush out of the wounds and spray her hand but, through a veil of tears, she saw a handful of dirt trickling out of the gash.

She knew with a terrible certainty it was the same type of wet soil Andy had vomited earlier. Puzzled, she polished off the bottle of vodka and pressed the scissors against her pubic bone. The bone offered no resistance, and she cut through it as though a piece of cloth. She continued cutting further up, all the way to the navel. A torrent of dirt came out like corn from a burlap sack; no inner organs, no slithering guts, just pure dark soil. Here and there, she saw pieces of trash, gum wrappers, plastic straws, expired bus tickets, crunched energy drinks. And in that flood of filth, there were words and sounds, whispers, but she couldn't understand them, like a dyslexic staring at a string of familiar yet mysterious symbols.

It kept coming, the flood of dirt as if her body was right

in the middle of an hourglass. Soon her feet and the coffee table were covered by a mound of earth. Then she heard the doorbell ring, and it sounded like a church bell. Tanya turned her deflated, crumpled face toward the door and, in a gravelly voice, said, "Come on in, mom, there's enough earth for a funeral."

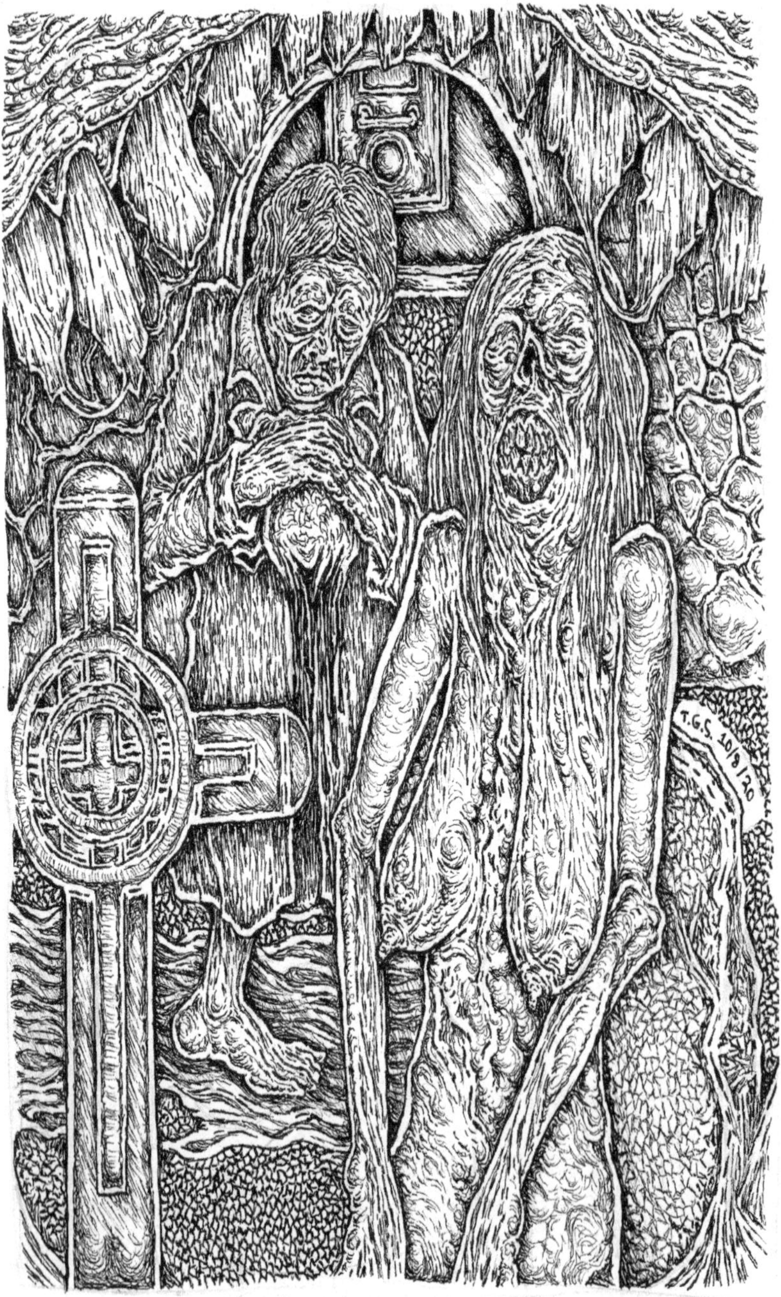
T.G.S. 10/8/20

THE PLAYGROUND WITH CROSSES

THE CRYPT WAS COLD; it smelled of cement and candles. I could not squeeze hugs from the rigid, dry hands. Through the iron bars of the window, I crawled outside and wandered around timidly. The cemetery: the playground of my childhood.

I ate weeds and drunk the cold milk of the marble crosses. After wandering around the whole day, in the evening, I went back to the crypt. I used to sleep huddled up on a dusty multicolored rug with tassels, laid on the bare cement, next to the shrinking body.

One day, while hugging a cross with all my strength, I saw a dog in the corner of my eye. It measured me with hungry yellow eyes. Its brown fur was rumpled, filled with thistles. It snarled and jumped at me savagely. I fell on my back, felt his teeth piercing brutally through my right arm, and I looked up at the clear blue sky. The cur chewed and ripped through my arm and then pulled it out of its socket. On a slide of screams, I tumbled into darkness.

I woke up. Through a veil of tears, I saw a bitch with saggy tits and purple nipples, crusts of bread on the ground, and pale women in black kneeling and wailing. I ate some funeral wheat porridge with my left hand and licked my fingers. I found a dusty black coat and a pair of old, muddy shoes in the chapel's back. I put the coat on and buttoned it up with shaky fingers. It smelled like a corpse. The shoes were big, heavy, and rough. I decided to walk barefoot.

I remember the day in which a grownup handed me a sack with something round and solid in it. He taught me how to kick it with my right foot. Once he left, I played with the sack for a while; I would kick it against the crumbling wall of a tomb, and it would roll back on the grass in front of me. Then I saw that the sack started bleeding—it left traces of blood in the dusty green. I lifted and opened it.

There was a woman's head inside. Her rumpled dark hair was greasy with fresh, sticky blood. I washed her at the pump and took her inside my crypt. Her facial bones were mostly undamaged, and she still had some shreds of skin on her ruined cheeks. Her eyes bulged, begging, unfocused, and frozen in resignation. In the evenings, I would kiss her on her decaying lips and fall asleep with her in my arms.

Then it rained for a long time. The crypt was humid and cold. Worms infested the head, and I had to toss it. I was so lonely and boring. I did not even know whether I was dead or alive. When finally the sun pushed through the bruised clouds, I wandered among the graves, speaking silently with every cross, caressing the oval sepia pictures with my pale fingers. One day, while I walked on the cemented alley in the middle of the cemetery and reflecting on the meaning of life, I stumbled and fell in a puddle.

In the trembling muddy water, I saw myself for the first time. My hair was dirty and ruffled. The corners of my mouth were turned down, like the mouth of a mourner. My eyes were vacant as the windows of a deserted house; two long shadows grew out of them—the open wings of a putrefied angel. My wrinkles were deep as if drawn them with a razor. My dirty, ashen skin was pulled tightly over my face, ready to rip and expose the skull beneath. I thought that if I carelessly fell asleep in an open casket, no one would believe I was still alive, that my heart still tossed about in my chest. They would bury me immediately, with no further discussion.

While I stared at my dreadful watery reflection, the wind started blowing, and my liquid face trembled and decomposed into small ripples. The wooden crosses' nervous screech accompanied the rusty, rhythmic screams of the metallic cemetery gates. Like broken wings, funeral wreaths rustled on the graves. Pushed from behind by a strong gust of wind, I ran down the alley towards the chapel. Then I felt I wasn't touching the ground with my feet anymore. I rose over the path. I looked down, and the puddles on the cemented pathway rushed away. On my sides, the branches of the trees quivered in the wind.

I was flying!

I shouted and cried with joy! I lifted my hand, caressed the crazy wind, and saluted the infinite skies. The wind lifted me even more. I looked down at the cemetery of my childhood and then up at the ocean of leaden clouds. I floated chaotically, my coat undulating in the wind and my legs moving slowly, like walking on air. I closed my eyes and felt an unfamiliar light sensation: I was smiling. Painfully, the corners of my mouth moved up, and my lips uncovered my blackened teeth. The down of the clouds gently caressed my wounded face, touches I had always dreamed of feeling. The warm kiss lasted just a few moments.

Then I opened my eyes and saw the grey cement speeding toward me. It hit me like a concrete fist. My skull broke like a putrefied cross. On a slide of fresh blood, I tumbled into darkness.

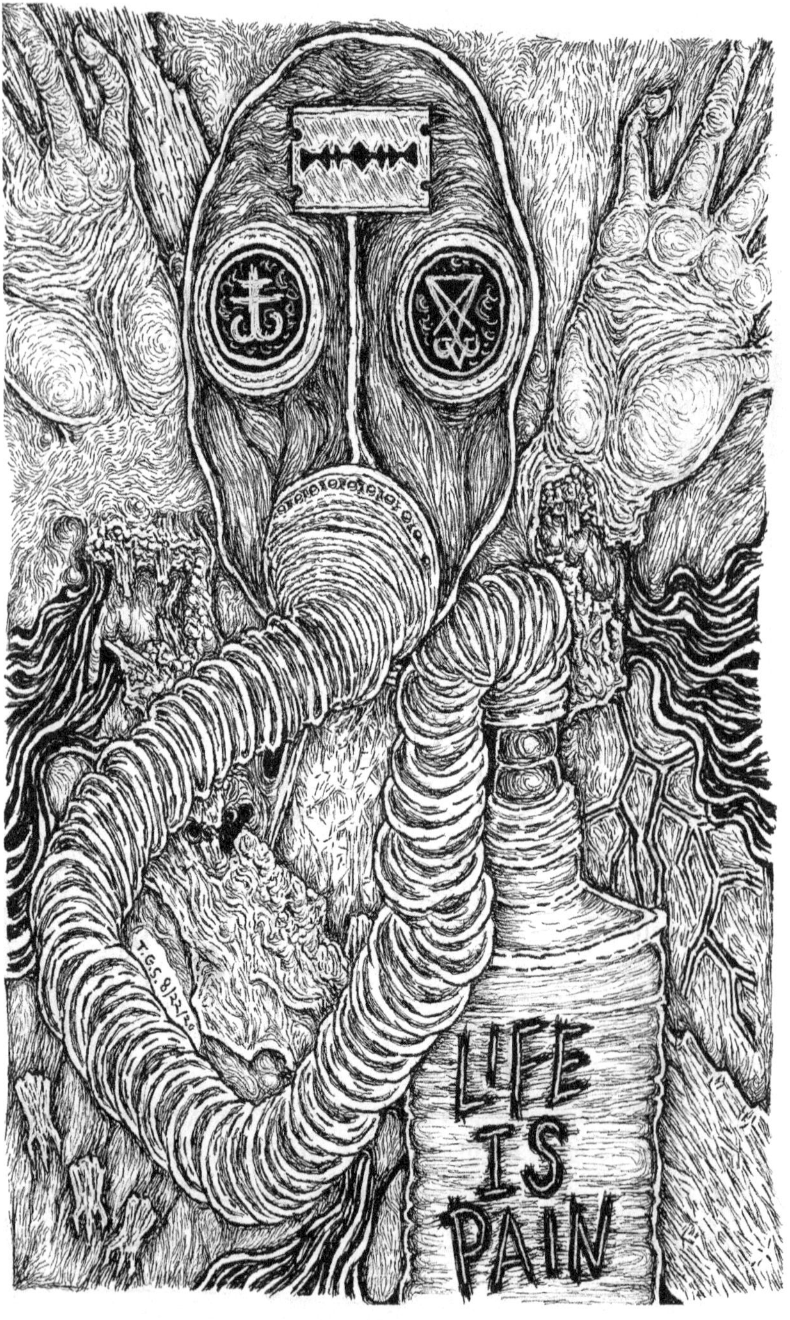
T.G.S. 8/22/20
LIFE
IS
PAIN

NATASHA SUICIDE

Natasha Suicide has lived up to her name. Or died up to her name to be exact; the anti-human, anti-life Russian beauty. I've met her on an online forum where she was avidly commenting about Depressive Suicidal Black Metal. Her beauty was stunning—elegant face, straight blonde hair, large green, intense eyes—but there was something alien hidden in those expressive eyes, like she was there but not really, like she could turn into the chick from The Exorcist at the flip of a switch.

When we'd chat from time to time she always threatened suicide and I knew she wasn't a poser, like the slut from Fight Club, feigning suicide just to get Brad Pitt's fat juicy cock. Natasha was the real deal. I mean, Russians are fucked! Ever heard of Chernobyl? She lived in a town just like that, some fucking Stalinist monotone industrial nightmare, Elektrovorsk or some shit. You don't need a nuclear disaster to want to die if you live there. Hell, you're basically born dead.

Speaking of Russians, have you seen the hoards of sick fucks, dressed in rags like zombies, who went to see Metallica and Pantera when they first played there after the fall of the

Iron Curtain? More than one million rockers came to the show in Moscow. Were those musicians on that stage or Gods descended from a leaden sky? Poverty breeds a special kind of metalhead, a true kind, a dangerous kind. But, back to Natasha, I lived in Canada and there wasn't much I could do to help her. And why bother anyway? Why help someone when you can sit back, study their self-destruction in slow motion, and wait for inspiration to strike.

When she abruptly deleted her Facebook profile I knew her time has come. She left the online world and probably the physical world as well. I found out the gory details later on from the list of internet comments spawned by her suicide. Yuliana, one of the nurses, was more than happy to spill the beans in exchange for social media attention. Natasha's suicide was probably big news in the small industrial town and fate placed Yuliana in the thick of the action. At first, I thought the nurse might exaggerate for dramatic effect but everything she reported aligned with my idea of Natasha's macabre style.

According to Yuliana, Natasha jumped from the tenth floor of her apartment building. Alas, she didn't die right away. Within minutes, they piled her skinny, broken body in an ambulance, and rushed her to the ER. She wore a gas mask on her face. Nobody knew why. One of the paramedics removed the mask and handed it to Yuliana as they reached the hospital. Even though agitated and shocked, Yuliana swore she saw strange black patterns on the mask's eyes, like satanic, occult symbols drawn with a marker.

Then the paramedic nodded toward Natasha, unable to speak. When she looked at the mangled body on the stretcher the nurse gasped; Natasha's head was all covered in duct tape, like a weird mummy, tufts of blond hair stuck out here and there, blood seeping through the gaps. Her black "Life is Pain" t-shirt and cut-off jeans were soiled with blood and barely held together a bony body. Her tiny bare feet were twisted at weird angles from her shinbones and knees. She looked like a doll suffering the vicious tantrum of an insane child in the middle of playing doctor.

No amount of practice prepared Yuliana for the sight. The norms of her training flashed in her mind like weird abstractions with no application to this gruesome reality.

Breathing.

First and foremost, they needed ensure the patient could breathe. Then they'd try to stop the massive bleeding and get a blood transfusion. Natasha could asphyxiate and choke on her blood with her mouth and nose sealed by duct tape. With trembling hands that seemed miles away, Yuliana grabbed a pair of scissors and started cutting through the gray mask. Soon, a gurgling sound came from deep inside Natasha's throat.

She was still alive.

Yuliana cut faster, all the way to the temple by Natasha's left eye. Blood stuck to the tape and scissors like jelly. When the nurse unglued the cover from her mouth, nose, and left eye, Natasha's jaw fell to her neck like an unhinged plate. A black thing coated in blood slid out of her mouth. It was her iPhone. The gore didn't penetrate its slick case. It appeared Natasha had pulled out her teeth and sliced the tendons of her jaw to fit the device in her mouth. The black earphones protruded from the jack, and black strings went to Natasha's ears.

She's still listening to music, Yuliana realized as a cold shiver went through her. Mechanically, she removed one of the earplugs. As if the nurse pressed the wrong button on a twisted robotic doll, Natasha began convulsing and screaming. Spit and blood flew from her exposed tongue. Except what came out of Natasha's throat, Yuliana insisted on clarifying, weren't really screams as much as the squeals of a stuck pig.

Natasha's left eye, the one not covered by duct tape, opened and stared at Yuliana, bulging with hatred. The green eye was tinged with pure red rage. The nurse said that she was suddenly, irrationally afraid for her life. As if the mangled, ruined body would somehow manage to pull itself together, get up, and chew on the fringes of her sanity. Rip at it with that horribly dislodged jaw.

Frantically, Yuliana replaced the earplug into Natasha's ear and the dying girl instantly stopped convulsing. The green eye squeezed shut and Yuliana swore tears roll out of it. But that might just be her bullshit. Then the dying girl's body was rocked by puking fits as a black, reeking substance gushed from her ruined throat, drowning the soiled phone. After that Natasha went still, a hideous doll. Nurses in white uniforms gaped at her, a faint vibration of sad music still spilling from her phone into her skull and the sudden silence of the ER.

The autopsy revealed Natasha had also ingested a lethal amount of pesticide before her jump, Yuliana was happy to share. Natasha wanted to be on the safe side, I thought, and do a thorough job. Suicide is a tricky business. Hitler ate a bullet, popped a cyanide pill, *and* had ordered his body to burn. Natasha was far worse than Hitler, trust me on this, although you won't find her name in history books. She hated *all* life and the pest of humanity. Knowing her enemy well, she strategized. Natasha knew the deceitful hideous thing, the chronic illness of being alive, would cling to her with its slimy limbs like a rejected and obsessive lover. She needed to battle it with all her strength.

Fight it till the end, fight it in style.

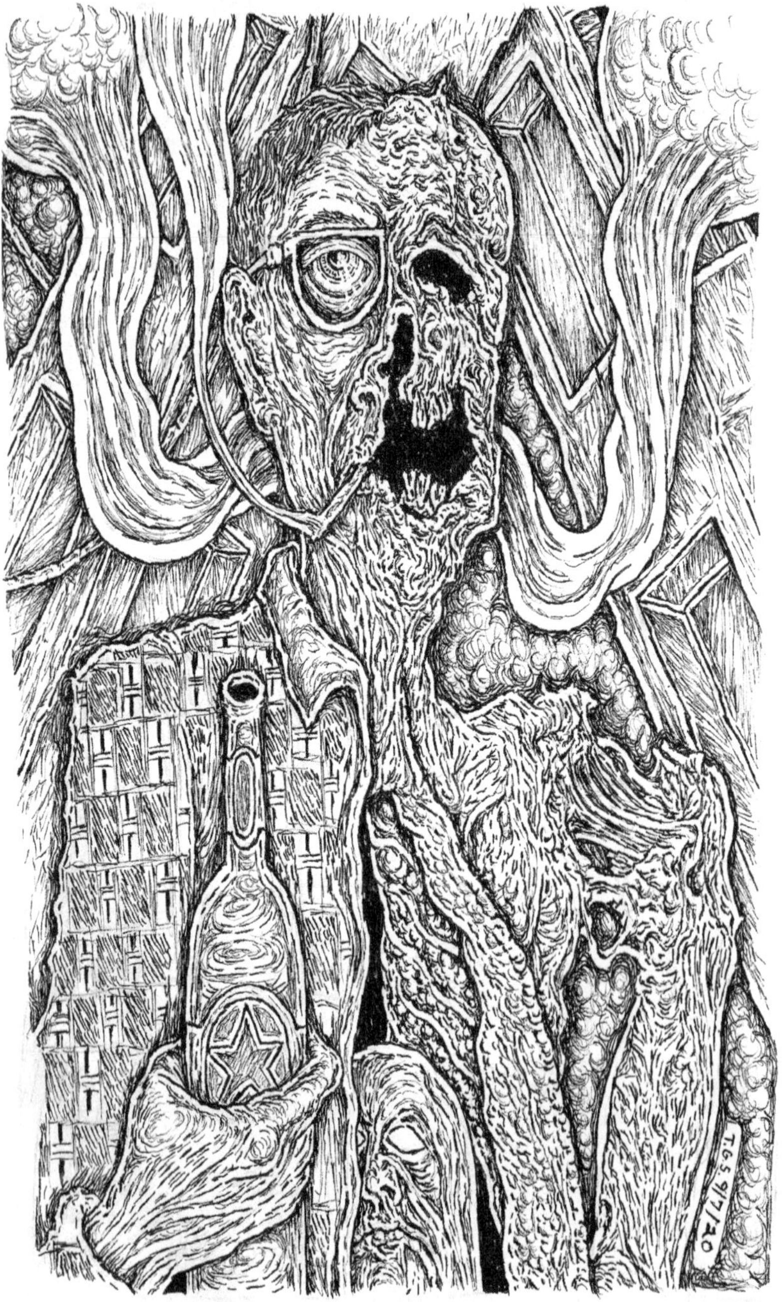
T.G.S. 9/7/20

FLORICA, THE LEGEND

I'VE MET Florica when I was in middle school. He was in this gang of metalheads my friends and I so desperately wanted to join. Back then, abusing alcohol was a way for us to look cool, extreme, and anti-social. It was a ticket into the club. Back then, there were no heavy drugs in small Romanian towns. But, looking back now, I realize that for Florica alcohol was more than a gimmick. He was a natural-born drunkard.

Florica wasn't very extreme or metal-looking but rather nerdy and quiet. He was short and stocky, always dressed in blue jeans and a neat plaid shirt buttoned up, with short, black hair and dark, intelligent eyes behind rimmed glasses. Already an avid smoker, he had a cavity build-up between his front teeth that showed whenever he smiled. His legend was firmly in place by the time I met him. He had already been in an alcoholic coma at least twice. The plunges into comas were preceded by the most erratic behaviour. The first time he crawled under a bench in the park where some metal girls sat. He licked their feet and their sandals' soles. The second time, at someone's place, he grabbed a leaf and started poking it against a light bulb while singing, *"Green leaf of fire, I'm hitting you against the light bulb."*

He was a fixture of The Penguin, the tavern that was our hangout at the time. He would be there when it opened and stay till closing or till we decided to hit another dive or go drink in the park across the street, always with his glass of vodka and his pack of cheap, unfiltered cigarettes. We could smoke in bars back then, and there were no ID requirements. The waitresses knew him well, and he told me once he had masturbated over every square inch of their asses.

At times he'd get philosophical and make references to Mircea Eliade or Emil Cioran, our intellectual idols. He told me how Eliade hated people trapped in sedating routines, always having their coffee at precisely the same time of day and so on, and how we should just go and knock over their cups and try to wake them up from their spiritual slumber. During these random anti-social outbursts, his eyes would glint with sadistic intent. His nervous involuntary blinking became more pronounced. His philosophical reflections were brief. He wasn't the type to rant about things for long. Once, he asked me out of the blue whether I thought that one could achieve spiritual enlightenment through the mortification of the body. Thinking of east Indian monks who live in meditation and eat dead bodies, I said yes.

Florica was always ready to get smashed. We were enrolled in different high schools, but since our town was small, we'd sometimes bump into each other in the morning on the way to school. More than once, we'd decide to skip class and get hammered. He'd either steal money from his parents or drink his class fund. Always vodka. Sometimes, when an important quiz was scheduled, I'd go to class and try to appear sober and hit the correct answers despite my double-vision. Then I'd stagger back to Florica's place to drink again. Often, we'd get plastered in the middle of a hot summer day, grabbing a bottle or two and wandering by the river valley in the unforgiving sun and passing out in a bush or under a tree.

Florica's love life was somewhere between Freudian lust and pure, idiotic romanticism. Once, he confessed he had made a move on his mom. His dad was away from home one night, and his mom suggested he slept on her bed as she was afraid to be alone. Florica saw this as an open invitation. Then, when the lights were off, he started caressing his mom gently through her soft nightgown, her shoulders and hips, and the lower side of her boobs. He told us he swore she started moaning when he fondled her nipples. This gave him confidence, and he whispered in her ear, "Do you want to make love?" The woman jumped out of bed as if it were on fire, turned on the lights, and shouted, "What did you say?" To which Florica replied meekly, rubbing his eyes, "Nothing, I was just sleeping."

One time, Mihaela's cousin Irina came to visit from Constanta. Mihaela was a pretty girl in our group, but her cousin was smoking hot, and Florica fell madly in love with her. When she went back to her hometown after a week or so, Florica decided to go after her and confess his undying love, become her slave if need be. Florica hopped on the train to Constanta, a five-hour journey, and halfway there, he realized he didn't know the girl's family name. She was Irina—that's it. Plus, Constanta was a big city with a few hundred thousand people. So, his romantic enthusiasm ended in bitter failure. He wandered the city for a couple of days and then headed back home, tail between his legs.

As you probably gathered, Florica was prone to erratic and absurdist actions, especially when drunk. One summer, we decided to go to this metal festival in a nearby town, hopped on the train, and proceeded to drink as per usual. After a few, Florica needed to use the washroom. On his way, he tripped over luggage in the aisle. Annoyed, he grabbed it and threw it out the window of the moving train.

The owner of the luggage missed the revolting action. When he discovered that his full duffle bag was gone, his suspicions naturally fell on us, as we were a group of rowdy young kids who wouldn't think twice before stealing. However, he had no evidence. He checked through our backpacks and found none of his items. His pack was lying in a field miles away by now. We said we knew nothing about his missing bag and looked at the floor, struggling not to burst out laughing. The guy looked like he was about to cry. He instinctively knew we were guilty but could not comprehend what happened. He eventually left us alone, defeated. Some of us felt bad for the guy and scolded Florica about it, but then we laughed it off and went back to drinking.

One summer evening, I went to Florica's *place, and* then we made our way to The Penguin. He seemed agitated and out of sorts and walked fast, a bit hunched over, smoking. I tried to keep up. He told me he'd been reading the first hundred pages of Dostoevsky's *Crime and Punishment* that day, and the story made him very anxious and unsettled. Then, when we were to crossed the street, he walked mindlessly into traffic, and I had to yell at him and pull him back before a car missed him by inches. He turned to me and gave me a strange smile, displaying the cavity on his front teeth. "Watch it, you idiot!!" I said, smiling back.

Florica died by getting hit by a car about fifteen years later. I was in Canada at the time, but I could imagine him walking fast, hunched over, a filterless cigarette dangling in his lips when the collision happened. I could hear the screech of tires and the thud of metal striking flesh and bone. I could feel the pain and the blood flowing as if it were my blood. As a teen, regularly drinking with a friend till you pass out is an act of communion that transcends time and space. Your friend bleeds. You bleed.

There are drunk drivers and drunk pedestrians. Many drunkards get hit by cars. Chronic alcoholism shrinks your brain and limits your attention—it atrophies your muscles, stiffens your limbs, and slows down your reflexes. But Florica knew all that, and he knew that even if the mortification of the body doesn't give you spiritual enlightenment, at least it might buy you the anti-hero role in a legendary story.

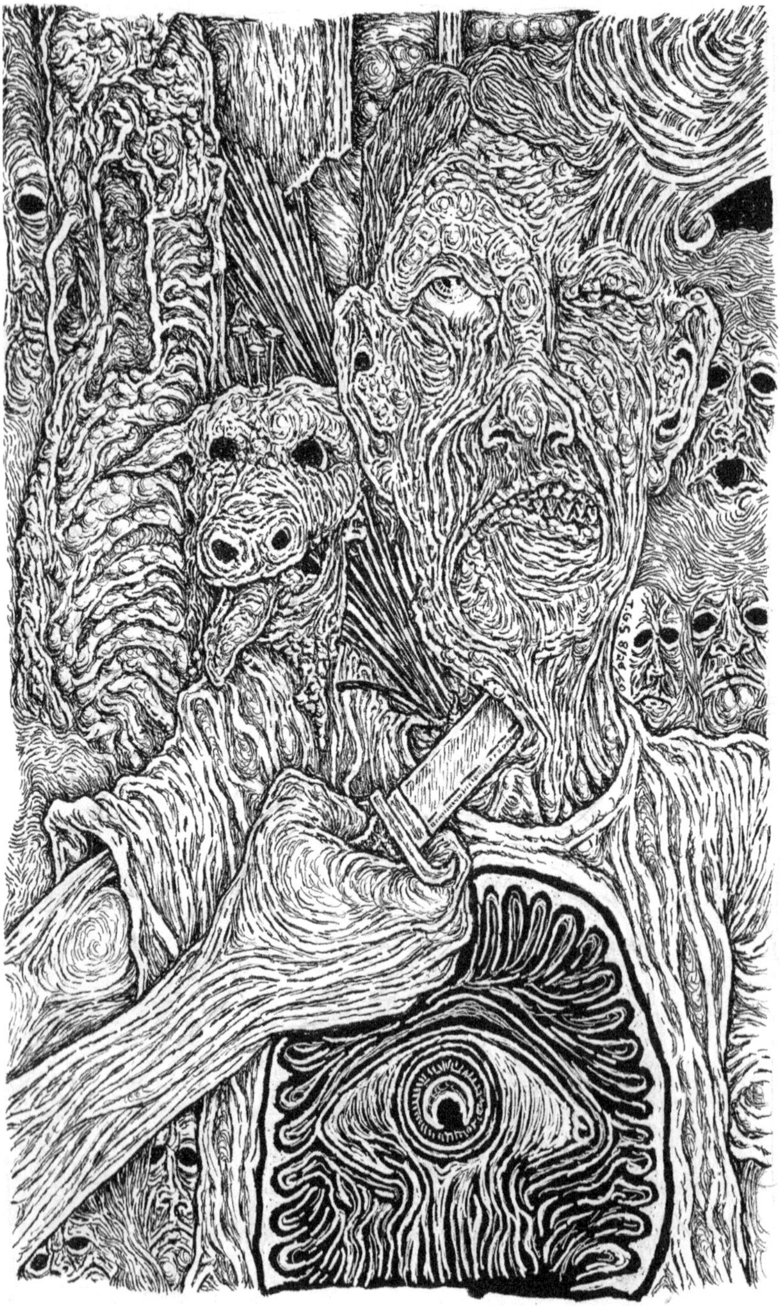

A PERFECT DAY

David was having a perfect day. His body buzzed with so much energy he felt like he could do anything. If he were a religious person, he'd have claimed it was a blessed day, but he hated that word, *blessed*. However, there was undoubtedly something mystical about it. Everything seemed so easy. At work, he made small talk with colleagues he usually avoided. He told Jack from receiving two Albertans hit the jackpot at Lotto 6/49. Jack was visibly pissed. He was an avid lottery player, and he answered that if he won the lottery, he'd buy a house with a big basement where he could play video games 24/7. Given his gargantuan size and grumpy manner, Jack was not a chick-magnet or a human magnet. David was unsurprised the troll harbored such escapist dreams.

None of the usual small, annoying accidents happened. David didn't drop any boxes of strawberries or mushrooms, didn't hit the skids full of produce against the empty stock carts or the stacks of merchandise arranged along the stockroom's sidewall, didn't bang his shins while using the fork pallet jack. A warm bubble wrapped him protectively. As if, after years of working in the tiny, cluttered, stinky stockroom, his brain finally calibrated the weight and behavior of all objects around him, and now it functioned in perfect harmony with its environment.

As he sipped his morning Starbucks coffee, David remembered this was a special day for other reasons too. It was payday. After work, he and Rose planned to buy their tickets for their Mexico vacation. He could almost smell the sea and the sand and taste the margaritas as he put the new stock away. Plus, he was close to hitting another 500 hours with the company, which meant another raise.

Moreover, Friday night meant Rose would get a rise out of him. She'd probably be extra-horny because of the exotic vacation. David smiled at the thought. On top of it all, the money he made today would go into their vacation fund. It was so great; he didn't remember the last time he'd felt so happy. Life burst with meaning.

During the lunch break, he talked to Rose. She worked at the cash register today. In the break room, he saw the glint in her eyes and her willing smile. She spoke of taking her four-year-old, Jordy, for his vaccinations, and how the doctor had been amazing. The doc sang a song to Jordy and poked him with his finger to make him laugh, so the lil' guy didn't even notice when the needle stuck. Then Rose went on about her fear of needles, and David stopped paying attention. He focused on the fine line of her neck, her lips, and the soft sway of her boobs through her shirt while she gestured. When she went to grab her coffee, he had a chance to admire her bubble butt. His mind swarmed with different sexual positions.

"But you're taking him to your folks tonight, right?" David asked anxiously when Rose sat back on the couch. Not that he disliked the lil' booger, but he was an attention-starved brat, and David wanted all the attention tonight.

"Yes," Rose answered and laughed knowingly.

David relaxed and offered a pleased smile.

After the lunch break, he finished putting the order away in the warehouse and went on the sales floor. It wasn't busy, so his mind was allowed to wander as he replenished the onions and potatoes, the lettuce and bell peppers, and cut corn with his knife. An old memory surfaced. He remembered the crazy doctor who had cut him with a scalpel when he had been in middle school. That summer, he went camping and helped gather wood for the bonfire. A splinter got stuck in the palm of his left hand, and David couldn't take it out, not all of it anyway. He paid no mind to the incident until, when back home, a little white spot appeared where the fragment was buried under his skin, and the area around it had turned an angry red. Then that white spot grew larger and larger and more painful. It got to the point he couldn't sleep at night, feeling the infection digging deeper into his flesh. He finally told his parents, and his dad took him to the hospital the next day.

The doc was an old bald guy with glasses and a hunched back. A portly nurse asked David to lie down on the bed, applied some brown liquid on the wound, and injected an anesthetic close to his wrist. The doctor came and sat next to him. He grabbed a scalpel from a tray, took David's left hand and stabbed the blade deep into his palm, and then pulled it out. Two vicious, expert motions. Blood and pus jetted up from the wound. David began screaming and crying and hitting the back of the merciless physician with his knees. His dad looked anxiously from behind the curtain and, unable to bear the screams, called David's mother at work.

When the quick procedure was done, the doctor left, and the nurse dressed the wound. She asked David had to come back the day after so the medic could check how the wound was healing and cut away the dead skin around it. David left the room on rubbery legs. Outside, he sat on a chair and cried. His mom joined his dad, and his parents looked at him sadly, helplessly. David felt like shit. He wore a metal t-shirt and was supposed to be a tough metal guy, but he cried like a pussy. David's mom tried to encourage him by saying he was as resilient as a pirate because he suffered surgery without anesthesia.

David didn't feel much like a pirate or anything. He felt humiliated.

Now, working on the floor, David ruminated on the memory and the antiseptic smell of hospitals, on how our parents can never really protect us from the pain. The memory didn't dampen his mood. He felt detached from it, like watching an entertaining movie in the theatre of his mind. He stayed happy and upbeat, talking to customers and offering smiles to everybody, his hands doing the job in a fast, methodical fashion. When his shift was over, he took the stock cart filled with empty boxes back to the stockroom. On the way, he saw the meat lady go outside for a smoke, and she asked him to look after her department for ten minutes. David agreed as he had experience working in meats, but, deep down, he knew he lied.

Ten minutes, that was enough to do it. David went to toss the empty boxes in the garbage and then looked around the receiving area. Jack wasn't there. No one was. Perfect. He stepped into the meat cooler. It was cold, but his hands were suddenly sweaty, and he felt dizzy, high on anxiety. He grabbed the knife from its leather sheath and, in a quick motion, stabbed it deep into his neck. Hard and savagely, like cutting through a steak.

Without hesitation this time.

David thought he almost heard the tip of the knife hit one of the cervical vertebrae. Then he slashed forward through his jugular, muscles, tendons, and arteries. Quick and fast, with surgical precision. Bright arterial blood and dark red venous blood splashed the shelves and the floor of the meat cooler. David was terrified, but he knew terror would come.

He didn't cry or scream but ground his teeth strong enough to crack his molars. A scream would alert them. Low, gargled growls came from his ruined throat. He was no longer a pussy like when he was as a boy. He was a Viking pirate. No cries, no ambulance, no paramedics. No more being manhandled and secured to a gurney. No complications, no regrets. Instinctively, his right hand went to his throat to stop the bleeding, but he moved it away, gloved in gore. There was no going back now.

Next, his knees turned to water, and he collapsed on the gray, concrete floor. The heart pumps five liters of blood in one minute, he thought. There are only five liters in a person's body. One other thought formed into his mind, but his oxygen-depleted brain couldn't read decipher it fully. Some regret—his parents weren't here to appreciate his courage and cheer him on. Then vague thoughts, sepia-colored memories; he knew all this and was prepared for it. The dull movie of his life. The tell-tale sign of his brain shutting down, the tiny projectionist passing out, drunk on his loneliness. A smile touched David's lips. He had done the hardest thing on the most perfect day.

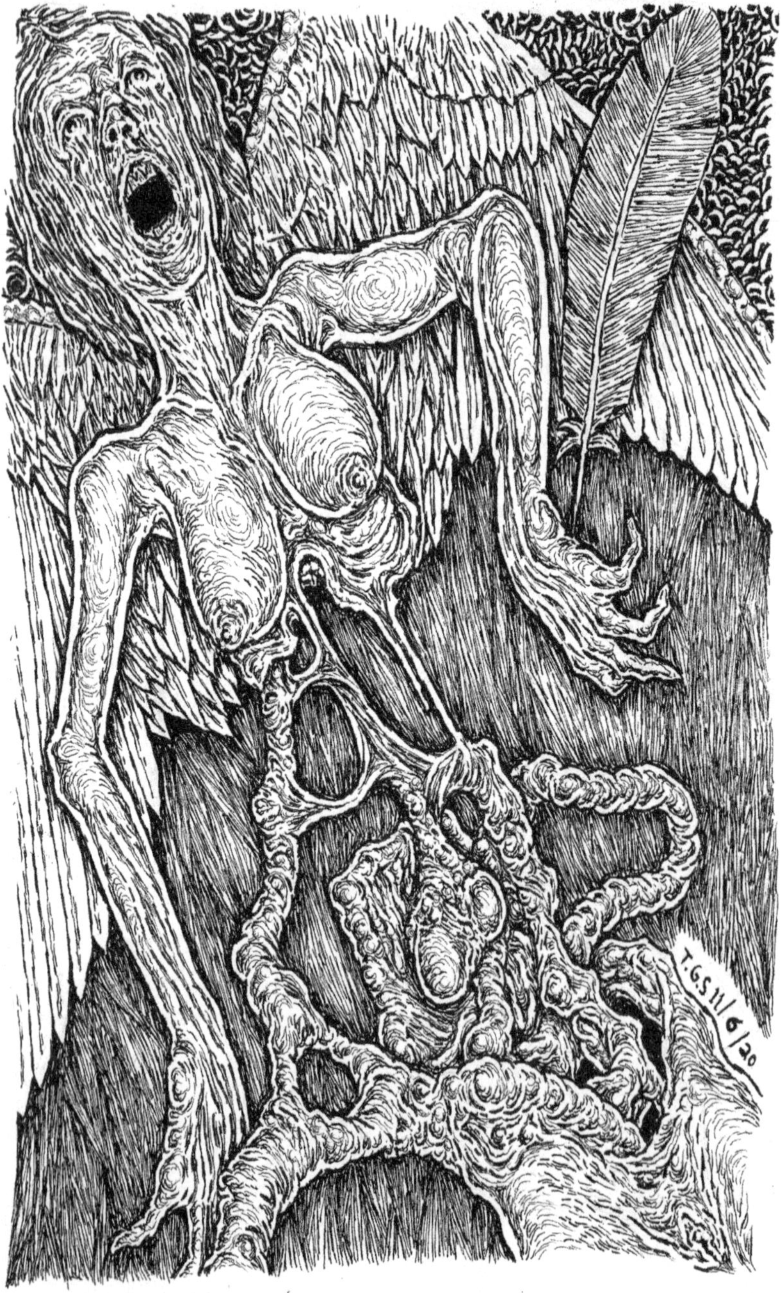
T.G.S 11/6/20

SUNDAY EXIT

I WAS READING my last poem when I saw Evelyn sitting at the top of the stairs leading to the bookstore's basement. I didn't recognize her at first as her hair was very short, probably because of the chemo, and she had lost weight. But I knew her when I observed her face, her posture, and her clothes, including her bag with the sign of the devil on it. I kept my focus and recited in a gloomy, monotone voice the lines of "Too Late for Suicide," to an audience of a dozen or so local poetry lovers that were already fully depressed; somewhat fitting for a Sunday afternoon.

> *Why stab a slug melting on the pavement?*
> *Why cut dried-up veins when blood is but a rusted*
> *   memory?*
> *Why blow your brains out when you can't smell*
> *   rotten burger meat or the blessed sulfur?*
> *Why hang yourself when the only time you breathe is*
> *   when you light a smoke?*

> *Here I am, committed to gray skies and empty*
>   *parking lots,*
> *the champion of leaf-clogged gutters, tumbled over*
>   *shopping carts, and broken toys,*
> *too tired to create something out of nothing,*
> *I'm convulsing like a sperm trapped in a bottle of*
>   *Prozac.*

Once done, I invited everyone upstairs for a book signing and a small reception. I fetched my backpack with copies of the book and then rushed to Evelyn.

"Hey, thanks for coming, long time no see," I said and gave her a warm hug.

"No problem," she said.

She was dressed in her usual Goth style: inverted cross necklace, a leather jacket, short black dress, fishnets, and black boots. She wore more makeup than usual and too much perfume. Her eyes were the same deep sky-blue, a bit clouded now, the eyes I had fallen in love with years ago. She had a small, elegant nose and a strong yet sensual jawline. The black amplified the paleness of her skin. The short hair reminded me of a young Sinead O'Connor.

"Do you want your copy signed?" I asked, noticing she was holding my book.

"Sure, but later. Go please your raving fans!"

I laughed, rushed up the stairs, and sat at a table by the entrance. I took out copies of my book and my pen while following Evelyn from the corner of my eye. First, a Goth guy with dark, round glasses came up to my table. He placed his copy in front of me. I noticed his black nails and makeup. His smile showed his plastic fangs. He said his name was Dagon and that Lovecraft based a story on him. He flashed his plastic smile again. I signed his copy and thanked him.

Then an unfortunate-looking woman blocked my field of vision. Her tiny porcine eyes were stuck in a doughy face, and she sported black, thick-rimmed glasses on her bulbous nose in an attempt at an intellectual look. Her gargantuan mouth looked like it could scarf down two dozen pancakes drenched in syrup in one sitting. An asymmetrical haircut and numerous tattoos were undoubtedly meant to deflect attention from her phenomenal proportions and project a sense of style. She gave me the book and I noticed her hairy hands and automatically thought of the bushes and forests covering her body. Her name was Crissy and she told me in a soft voice she found my poetry soothing, especially when she was feeling blue. I figured if she tried to hang herself in her apartment the entire building would collapse before she turned blue. I laughed privately at the thought. Then I signed the book and thanked her.

When the unpleasant ritual of book-signing was done, I placed the leftover copies in my backpack, grabbed a glass of wine, and went to talk to Evelyn. She was chatting with Dagon about the Edmonton Goth scene.

"I don't go to any shows," Dagon declared. "I dislike people unless they're my slaves. I rarely make appearances like this, but when I do it's mostly to hunt new victims." He displayed his fangs and hissed.

Evelyn looked at me and rolled her eyes.

Dagon had his earphones in his hands and I recognized the sorrowful piano notes of a familiar song. "Is that Gloomy Sunday?" I asked.

"Yup," Dagon confirmed. "I listen to the Hungarian Suicide Song every Sunday. I'd go there to kill myself but, unfortunately, I'm a vampire and, thus, immortal."

"I like Emily Autumn's version, with the violin," Evelyn said.

"I wonder if more people jump from the Golden Gate

Bridge than the Chain Bridge in Budapest," I mused and rubbed my chin.

"I imagine Sunday gloom is a universal disease," Evelyn noted.

Dagon polished his wine and said, "Unfortunately, my friends, I need to depart. The minions of my cult are waiting and then I have a D&D session." To me, he said, "I will read you melancholy book, sir, and I'll send one of my ravens with my thoughts for you."

I thanked him and smiled.

Once Dagon was out the door Evelyn and I looked at each other and burst out laughing. She reflexively covered her mouth. "That's one way to make an impression," she said. Then she looked at me with a glimmer of joy in her eyes, "The last line in your poem, 'a sperm trapped in a bottle of Prozac'? Never heard that one before."

I looked around to make sure there were no readers within earshot before I answered, "Yeah, like who would cum in a bottle of Prozac when there's so many good socks out there?"

We both laughed and she covered her mouth again. This time I glimpsed the reason: her yellowed teeth and blackened molars. Back when we dated her teeth were perfectly white and healthy, so I wondered if the decay was an effect of chemo, too much smoking, or both.

"Thanks again for coming", I said. "I noticed you signed up for the event on Facebook, but you know how it is...who actually shows up is a different story."

"You're welcome," she said. "I've meant to see you for a while."

"The short hair suits you," I pointed out.

"Yeah, it's fine like baby hair."

She skimmed through my book. "Too late for suicide? I say, better late than never." She gave a yellow smile and looked deep into my eyes, "I tried to off myself," she confessed from out of the blue. "I'll do better next time. It's a learning process." This simple statement, its candid desperation, made me turn to stone, overwhelmed by irrational guilt and embarrassment. I knew she had rectal cancer and wore a colostomy bag. And I knew I would have killed myself had I been in her position. However, it was weird her telling me that. She knew I wasn't into comforting people.

My outlook had always been pessimistic. I advocated suicide. I was never part of the *Live-Love-Laugh* crowd. So, what was the point? Was she saying she was cool now? Totally in agreement with me, ready to be part of my Suicide Club?

There was a subtext my brain struggled to decipher.

"I'm sorry," I mumbled.

She sensed my uneasiness and patted my shoulder. "Hey, such is life, shit happens." She laughed a bit too loud with a healthy dose of hysteria.

"Overdose?" I asked. I knew Goths were all gimmicks in their worship of death. When the time came, they didn't have the guts to cut down through their forearms as through steak or cleave their heads with a shotgun blast. No way! They'd either scratch their wrists or take five sleeping pills with 911 on speed-dial.

"Yeah, bad idea. Trial and error. I half-assed it too." She smiled and winked at me.

That wink was a clear signal. "Do you wanna hang out at my place? You drive?"

"Sure," she accepted immediately. "Of course I drive, you're still hoping the loser cruiser?" She nudged my arm teasingly.

"Hey, I'm still a starving artist," I said and opened the door of the bookstore for her. "And you know what Cioran said, all that counts in this world is being the loser."

"You and your Cioran," she said and rolled her eyes.

Evelyn and I have dated in our early twenties but it didn't last. We were both ambitious but wanted different things. She wanted money and I wanted to be a poet. She went into business school and then banking. When her salary reached six figures—while I lived in squalor on minimum wage—and she realized the world was her oyster, she dumped me in a heartbeat and shelved all her artistic and intellectual projects that gave meaning to our relationship. Since then, I hadn't seen her in about six years—but knew about her fight against rectal cancer from Facebook.

She drove a red VW Beetle that was parked close to the bookstore. A stench of weed assaulted my nostrils as I got in. "So, you use weed as a painkiller?" I asked as I fastened my seatbelt.

"Yeah, it puts me to sleep too, the forgetting is kinda cool, more exciting than remembering" She laughed nervously. "You're still in that shitty apartment by Southgate?"

"One and the same," I said. "I have more books since the last time you visited."

"Bookworm," she teased.

She put on Katatonia and the melancholy music amplified the desolation of the city. Edmonton, aka Deadmonton, aka The Place Where Feelings Come to Die, was sleeping away its hangover after a tumultuous Saturday night and bracing for another week of nine to five. Under a gray sky tinged with the red of dusk, the downtown area was animated mainly by hobos, junkies, prostitutes, and the religiously exalted. We passed a bum carrying a big bag of bottles in a stroller, probably aiming for the next bottle depot. Another one sat on the sidewalk with a bag of Doritos next to him and was methodically smashing the chips into powder.

At a corner, a prophet was shouting in a megaphone about sin and salvation, perched on an upside-down milk crate. Strategically placed near a McDonalds, another hobo held a curt sign: "Jobless, homeless, hungry." At the 7 Eleven on Jasper Ave. there was a police car parked near a group of Aboriginal Indians, one of them collapsed on the pavement.

I pointed the store to Evelyn, "I went inside there once and there was a note on the slushy machine, 'Don't put alcohol in slushies.'"

Evelyn glimpsed at the seedy location and grimaced, "Edmonton is a classy city, no doubt about it."

Down 109st we passed the High Level Bridge and headed to Southgate Mall where we stopped to get drinks and pizza. At Wine and Beyond we made our usual jokes with the clerks: me asking for the "beyond" section and Evelyn asking for their "finest" ten-dollar wine.

When we got to my place, I put everything on the coffee table in the living room and then went to the kitchen to open the first wine bottle, get a wine glass for Evelyn, and plates and napkins for the pizza.

Murky sunset light and a slight breeze came through the balcony door. I turned on the light.

She placed her bag by the coffee table, her jacket on the couch, and began browsing through the books that lined the opposite wall. Her round and firm buttocks' contours were evident under her short black dress, and my heart sank as I realized anal was off the table. Vivid memories of taking her from behind assaulted my brain and I felt my erection press against my jeans.

At the top of a stack of books, Evelyn found my gun, my Glock 22. She showed it to me and raised an eyebrow.

"That's my insurance policy," I explained, "my pension plan." *Just in case I get ass-cancer*, I thought to myself. "*The blessed smell of sulfur*," I quoted my poem out loud.

"You know gunshots don't release sulfur? Unless you live in the eighteenth century and use black powder."

"Really? Oh, shit! I messed up my poem." I covered my face with my hands.

"Do your research, lazy bones," she said as she continued to handle the gun.

She pressed the muzzle to her temple and rolled up her eyes deep in her head.

"You should watch it. It's actually loaded."

"Really? That's exciting."

She aimed the gun at me, a playful smile on her face.

I pointed to my head. "You should pretend I'm a zombie and shoot me in the head. I don't want to suffer too much."

"Pretend?" she asked, cocking an eyebrow. "I *know* you're a zombie. I've read your poetry. And also, zombies don't suffer, you meathead."

I dropped down on my knees in front of her. "Oh God, I'm worthless and can't even kill myself."

She laughed and covered her mouth. I stood up and kissed her, decayed teeth and all, the gun between our beating hearts. Pleased with the kiss, she placed the pistol back on the shelf with a kind of reverence and sat on the couch.

I set the open wine bottle and the glass in front of Evelyn and the plates by the hot pizza. Then I opened the laptop and allowed her to continue the day's soundtrack on YouTube. I knew Katatonia, Chelsea Wolfe, and Anathema would make up the mournful playlist. I plopped in the armchair and popped open my first beer as she filled up her glass of wine. She took a big gulp and began spilling her guts about her rectal cancer with the intensity of all people who went through hell and lived to tell the story. "You know me, how I used to be...I always thought of myself as a winner, hungry for success, hungry for life, always in competition, focused, full of my own will. And, when I was diagnosed, I thought I could beat this cancer...with my healthy outlook and positivity... And all the doctors were very supportive, this was just routine stuff for them. They assumed you wanted to fight it. 'Assuming' makes an ass out of you and me." She gave a strained laugh.

This reminded me of a recent grisly incident. "I know how it is, this guy jumped in front of a train at the Southgate station...a few weeks ago. One of my friends knew him, it was this teen suffering from chronic depression. Anyway, he didn't die right away but was cut in half and they tried to keep him alive in the hospital with surgeries and everything. But why on earth would they try to save him? The guy didn't want to live in a normal body. What makes you think he'd want to live cut in half? Just let the poor soul go."

Evelyn said, "Jumping in front of a train? That's pretty extreme. There might be some Christian beliefs at work in the background. You know the stigma associated with suicide, the doctors or family members probably think that by saving your body they save your soul or some nonsense like that."

Evelyn finished her first glass of wine, poured a new one, and continued her lamentations. "I guess I beat cancer, for now anyway, but it's a bitter victory. It just turned out to be too much, my freedom vanished, and everything revolves around shit, crap, poop, excrement. It's different when you shit through your stomach than through your ass. Now I'm so envious of people who can poop naturally. Normal people can go through a day without thinking about shit at all. But a bag attached to your stomach is more difficult to ignore. You have to change it many times a day and you can't help but see your shit, smell it. You develop a more intimate relationship with excrement. Am I grossing you out?"

"No," I lied automatically. "This actually gives me an appetite," I joked and fetched the first slice of pizza.

She smiled knowingly. "In the end, I decided I wanted no part of this. Living for the purpose of living, forming a deep spiritual connection to your excrement. The gift of life, some say. Well, I'll happily return that gift...or regift." Nervous chuckling. "Thanks but no thanks! And going to regular appointments to see if cancer has spread or not. Have you ever heard of barium enema? I hope you never do. They inject a metallic liquid into your intestine... Not fun! Also, never trust nurses when they say something is just 'a bit uncomfortable.' It's probably torture. No, fuck that noise! This gave me some fucked-up nightmares too. In the dream, I was being raped on the sidewalk and the guy's cum felt like rough cement that turned into concrete inside me. And I had wings, long, white wings and I struggled to fly away. He was still at my back, chuckling and mocking my efforts. And I started beating my wings harder and harder, in a frenzy, and I finally managed to fly away. I felt so happy for just one moment. Then I looked down and saw my guts hanging. I had struggled so hard I ripped myself in half. Blood splashed on the sidewalk from my hanging guts and I realized I'll pass out and die soon from blood loss. I woke up as my head cracked against the pavement."

"That's a fucked-up dream," I said as I placed the grisly imagery in the working memory box in my brain. "What happened to your job?"

"My job? Well, I got the chemobrain, you know, fogginess, forgetfulness, ADD. I could barely focus on anything. I'll have this problem all my life. I can't escape, read a book, watch a movie, play a video game. It's like you're imprisoned in a shitty situation, pun intended. Obviously, as a result, my work suffered. I feel they kept me on out of pity. I became a charity case. Thank you, universe!" She put her hands together in mock prayer.

Evelyn polished her glass of wine and poured another one. She was so eager to get drunk she drank the booze like water. That was fine by me as every time she filled a new glass, I could gaze down her large cleavage and remember her perfect, milky white boobs.

She asked, "Do you get the impression that this world has become a large support group? It's like you have to live no matter what. People told me to make social media accounts and connect with others who are going through the same thing and receive support from them and helpful tips, etcetera. So, the question is not what you want to do with your life. Just being alive is a good enough goal. A generation of losers is what this is.

"Here's your participation trophy for playing the game of breathing. Early on, I liked studying business and making money. I was good with numbers and enjoyed helping a business grow, enjoyed being wealthy and successful, buying nice things, you know how I was. But it was never my ambition to beat rectal cancer. I wanted no part in that story. Cancer turned my life upside down and made me re-evaluate everything. I mean, you know, I was always self-centered but also wanted a family. I don't want to be some bitter careerist like the bitch from *The Devil Wears Prada*. End up paying for sex. I was always a chooser, not a beggar. Fuck that noise! I thought for a while I should stay alive to be there for my pets. Or to become the cool aunt if my brother decided to have kids. Or help my parents in their old age. And become some crazy cat lady. But Ruby, my guinea pig, died last week. Pets just die on you, there's no point. And my brother is probably gay and I don't feel much for my parents; they're all set in British Columbia, plenty of good retirement homes. I just don't have the energy. Cancerous kid taking care of senile parents. Too sad, too sordid."

She looked at me with teary eyes and I gave her a cold smirk. "Women, always needing to care for something. That's just your maternal instinct. It's kinda ridiculous having nothing better to do than caring for some dumb pets. Like all these women posting pictures of their 'furry babies' on Facebook, it's sickening."

"I take it you're still single? I wonder why? You're so full of empathy and kindness." She raised an eyebrow as a challenge.

I guess I got a bit defensive and started dropping names again, "You know, Schopenhauer said women are somewhere between children and men."

"Oh, I see you're still masturbating by quoting misogynistic philosophers. Definitely single." She made stroking gestures in the air.

"I know a few cheap escorts. That's what I spend my money on, books and prostitutes."

"Classy! Why are you so bitter, did they give you syphilis like they did that incel, Nietzsche?"

"No, tests came back negative. And to be clear, I'm not a misogynist, I'm a misanthrope, I hate both men and women equally."

"Is that so?" she asked.

"Yup."

"But you just happen to have your group of misogynist philosophers you always defer to?"

I shrugged, a bit uncertain. Evelyn's interrogations were always a mix between Socratic dialogues and the Spanish Inquisition. Her hardened face and tightly pressed lips indicated she was in full judgmental mode.

"So, just wondering, do you also have a woman you happen to admire?"

This made me think. Not much came to mind. I wanted to say, *my mom*, but that was a bad joke. *Women I admire? Writers? Philosophers?* Suddenly it came to me. "I think Sylvia Plath is very cool," I said with a sigh of relief. "*Dying is an art, like everything else—*"

"—*I do it exceptionally well*," Evelyn finished the famous verse. She nodded, relaxing. "Good answer."

Pleased, I added, "And I don't mind you either."

"Oh, thank you," she said batting her lashes.

"Speaking of which, your boyfriend left you?"

"Dumped me like a sack of potatoes as soon as the cancer news came. I'm over it though, water under the bridge. I mostly kept him for sex anyway. He was an idiot otherwise."

Evelyn excused herself to go to the washroom. As I cracked open the fourth beer, I realized I was pleasantly tipsy. I definitely enjoyed Cancer-Evelyn more than Driven-Evelyn. I could only socialize with people who more or less gave up hope. Or regarded any hope with irony or skepticism. This meeting had a surreal vibe to it. Our attachment to life was so fragile, we almost seemed to inhabit a ghostly dimension, somewhere in the waiting room of Purgatory, sharing some earthly stories and memories. We were also on a plane of eternity, so resigned that we were completely free, so powerless we were godly. A sacred space, a dream space, where anything could happen.

Back on her couch, she poured another glass of wine, took a big gulp, and continued. "This 'battle' with cancer took too fucking long and changed me... All this hero/warrior bullshit is a cover, a scream of agony, something to divert my attention from the fact I'm just trembling flesh, waiting for a blurry salvation...I realized I'm nothing. There is nothing to gain, nothing to wait for. Being a survivor is the lowest stage of human evolution. Why survive? Suicides are always more enlightened than the survivor-types. The weak always repeat their mantras: 'what doesn't kill you makes you stronger,' or 'it's a trial from God.' I can't shrink my brain enough to believe that bullshit."

"You know that's from Nietzsche, what doesn't kill you

makes you stronger. That's before Kelly Clarkson gayed it up. I imagine it sounded edgier in the nineteenth century."

"Yeah, now there's this meme: what doesn't kill you makes you have unhealthy coping mechanisms and a dark sense of humor."

"That sounds more truthful," I agreed.

"All the other women on those social media support groups talked about their 'battle scars' and 'tiger stripes' and how this is a trial from God to make you humble. The Book of Job kinda stuff. Except I've always been prideful. What's wrong with that? Satan is the symbol of pride and arrogance." She held her necklace and stuck her chin out as if defying me to answer.

"Christians are all enchanted with the Book of Job but all it shows is that God has a gambling problem. He bets on how long his minion can withstand torture." We both laughed at that.

Then she became reflective again. She was talking so much and seemed so strained that I wondered how long since she spoke to anyone. A few days? A full week or two? I plucked out a joint from my pack of cigarettes. I had rolled it earlier that day. I lit it and took a deep drag, filling my lungs. I passed it to Evelyn. Slowly a bluish haze filled up the room.

Evelyn passed me the doobie and said, "It's an uphill battle to unglue these labels they stick on you, all these band-aids like 'cancer survivor,' 'warrior,' 'battle-scars.' And the labels are more useful for them than for you, helps them move on with their lives. What I find under the labels is nothing, just silence, and darkness. There's no 'I', some person with a unified center. Evelyn Douglas. See, they started lying to us since we were kids. *All naming is lying.* 'I' is no more real than Santa or God. Even saying your self is 'fractured' is a lie. 'Fractured' assumes it was once whole, but we're never whole. We always see the darkness but are trained to ignore it, just like you become numb to all the homeless people you see on your way to work. But once you see that darkness, once you stare it in the face, fully focused, no distractions, once you fully grasp that emptiness, then there's nothing left to do because you are no more. You're just 'It.' You know, 'It' from 'It happens' or from 'Shit Happens.' I kinda had to pull myself back together to try to kill myself. I had to pretend I existed so I could then not exist."

For lack of something better, I quoted my poem again. "*Here I am, committed to gray skies and empty parking lots/ the champion of leaf-clogged gutters, tumbled over shopping carts, and broken toys.*"

"I know," she said. "*Sperm trapped in a bottle of Prozac.*"

"That's me," I admitted.

She took one last hit from the joint and stubbed it in the ashtray. "The desolate imagery in your poem reminds me of my Chernobyl nightmares. I must have watched some movies about the Chernobyl disaster and associated it with radiation therapy. I'm just hovering over the dead city, over these gray cubical empty buildings, the feral vegetation, the empty parks, the communist murals... I just feel gloom and impending doom. And then I look up at the sky and all I see is this giant gray spaceship. Kinda like the one in that movie *District 9*." Evelyn stopped and rubbed her chin. "Except maybe it's not a spaceship but this gray massive structure, like an upside-down pyramid...but you don't see its base, it's all in the clouds. And I feel suffocated, trapped. There's no sky above, just this suspended alien construction. So I start climbing this structure like an insect, and it's just this mass of pure dread, each level larger and more foreboding than the next. I feel damned like Sisyphus, I know it's in vain but I keep trying, keep climbing."

Evelyn stopped and filled another glass of wine with a shaking hand. "One night I woke up after this recurring nightmare and felt my side was wet. Sure enough, my stoma was leaking. I literally shit the bed. And the stench was putrid. Woke up from one nightmare into another. I'm an abandoned city so poisoned with radiation it can no longer support life." She stared into space for a few moments, as if briefly paralyzed by the dark memory.

"I too have some crazy dreams. I think you know my mom suffers from dementia and is in a senior's home?"

She shook her head. "Sorry to hear."

I shrugged. "I visit her at times, she has that constant frown on her face as if struggling to remember something. She barely moves, just sits on her chair, eats and gets fat, watches TV without really understanding anything. Anyway, I had this nightmare that a band of feral kids invaded the home and started throwing stones at her and she began screaming and talking gibberish, her eyes wild like those of a cow at slaughter. And the kids laughed at how she was so slow and fat and making weird noises."

"That's terrible," Evelyn said.

"Well, it was a nightmare. They tend to be terrible," I jested.

"I can't live with no goals, in this kind of phantom-state, just killing time," Evelyn said, going back to her deep sorrow. "I see myself a few years from now on a long Sunday afternoon, with a big stack of movies and video games, in a filthy room smelling of cat piss and rotten farts, fat on a big couch, looking to order a new dildo on eBay. I prefer not to, you know what I mean? Thanks, life, but no thanks. It's like the engine won't start anymore and I don't know where I'm going. There is a strike inside my head. The workers refuse to engage." She tapped her index against her temple. "And as the workers stop, I see things for what they really are. All that work, the hustle and bustle, it's all smoke and mirrors—magical thinking to give the impression something's happening. But nothing's going on; I'm just meat floating through the void, spoiled meat flung into the abyss... Actually, all meat is spoiled, but you know what I mean. And that's when I thought about you...your writing...you always thought that... But I don't really care anymore. I don't know." She finished her monologue with a shrug and sat back on the couch like a dejected child.

I knew I was right but took no pleasure in it. There's no prize to be won by those who truthfully note that life is but pointless suffering, a cosmic meat-grinder. However, I took a small amount of pleasure from the fact that she remembered me. Without cancer and its effects on her, I probably wouldn't have seen her again. Hanging out with Evelyn again was neat, in a tragic way. For old time's sake, as they said.

I got up from my chair and fetched Cioran's *A Short History of Decay* from my library. "What you said about Sunday reminded me of this epic passage: 'The universe transformed into a Sunday afternoon...it is the very definition of ennui, and the end of the universe.'"

Evelyn rubbed her chin thoughtfully. "Is ennui the same as spleen or malaise?"

"Exactly. I think it comes from Baudelaire's *Les Fleurs du Mal*. Cioran defines it early on." I turned the pages to the beginning of the book, looking for passages I underlined. "Here it is, 'Ennui makes us find time long, too long—unsuited to show us an end. Detached from every object, having nothing external to assimilate, we destroy ourselves in slow-motion, since the future has stopped offering us a *raison d'être*. Ennui shows us an eternity which is not the transcendence of time, but its wreck; it is the infinity of souls that have rotted for lack of superstition, a banal absolute where nothing any longer keeps things from turning in circles, in search of their own Fall. Life creates itself in delirium and is done in ennui.'"

"That sounds cool. My take on Sundays is they should be outlawed." She gave me a yellow-toothed smile. "You and your master Cioran, I knew you'd get me."

I placed the book back on the shelf, had a deep drink of beer, and said, "Well, you've been through more shit than me, pardon the pun, but there's still something common to our suffering. I just live out of habit. I like books and writing, but I have no deep-seated commitment to myself or this world. You know how my mom, ever the practical woman, was fully opposed to me studying English and becoming a writer? Once, in a heated argument, she said, 'I made you, I kill you.' I thought it would be cool to go to her senior's home and give her my gun, kneel in front of her senile face and beg her to kill me. I think this is ironic. There's a poem in there somewhere. That dementia face though, almost a mask. Her eyes are grayish, clouded over; I know she struggles to recognize me most of the time. I tell her these stories and she has no reactions, just staring at me. At times her dentures pop up of her mouth and then she sucks them back in like chewing gum. I get tired and exhausted very quickly."

"Dementia is the pits! It sucks when they forget their own names. My parents are starting to have it too."

I polished up my beer and opened another can. "Speaking and thinking are defense mechanisms, delaying tactics. I feel like someone watches silently inside my head, a somber, hard look like one of those statues from Easter Island. At times, as I wait at the bus station, it's watching me from the vault of my cranium, just there, stony-faced, quietly judgmental and malignant. I instinctively start spinning a story about where I'm going. It says nothing, just stares me down intensely, from the center of that oppressive silence. That's the quiet before the storm, before the great flood. Just like you said, that black stillness fucks you up. I wish I could cover myself with the blanket of just one thought, sleep and rot, forget the trauma of time and movement.

"But my thoughts scurry away like frenzied rats in a maze. While waiting for the bus, I start telling myself dumb shit about random things, like 'I got this pair of shoes for cheap,' or 'Look there! A dentist's office right by my place,' or 'The grass is vibrant green, what a nice summer.' Cause I know that if I shut up I die, I melt away. I swear to god, at times, when the bus is late, I feel like I'm gonna crumble under pressure. I become so tired I can barely move. I collapse under the force of that stare. It's always there, more or less. When I finally see the 'loser cruiser' around the corner I want to scream with joy and hug that driver for being my hero.

"On a good day I manage to forget about it and focus on the business of killing time, playing the poet, ordering books, writing and commenting and critiquing. But it knows I'll run out of steam and start begging for the bullet eventually. I feel like a buffoon trying to entertain a lethargic king and running out of jokes."

I finished my beer, set the empty on the table, and belched loudly.

Evelyn had a smirk on her face. "You're sure running your mouth a lot, so you must be very afraid. Also, buy a car!"

I smirked and shook my head. "I'm made of fear, paradoxical dread, fear of everything and nothing. Owning a vehicle would make me even more anxious and depressed. So many things to look after, so many chances to die."

She nodded knowingly and looked down. The alcohol in my bloodstream and all this talk of death and spoiled meat made me horny. Plus, my brain was tired of bleak abstract ramblings and craved a distraction. If I managed to ignore the little bulge with the bag, Evelyn was as hot as ever. I checked her out more directly and whistled in appreciation. "So, you think you're just a piece of meat?"

She looked at me with a glint of desire. "A piece of shit, to be exact."

"I'd fuck you for free."

"Oh yeah?" She raised an eyebrow in challenge.

Then I spit on her face. The glob of phlegm hit her right eye. Her left eye went wide and her chin trembled a bit. I stood up quick and slapped her. Some of the spittle spread to the edge of her nose.

"Okay, you piece of meat, kneel now and suck!" I said in an authoritative voice I knew Evelyn couldn't resist. One thing about Evelyn was that beneath her feminist posturing she was perfectly submissive. She was normally such a control-freak that relinquishing her power was a perfect blessing. She was one of those progressive Satanists who thought being kinky was a way of attacking God and the patriarchy. I didn't know how that ideological battle was going, but I knew she wanted sex from the moment I saw her at the bookstore, all dolled up for me.

She quickly got on her knees, opened my zipper, and started to suck obediently. I got fully hard fast. I grabbed her head and pressed it deep against my crotch till she gagged. Her short hair made the idea of skull-fucking more vivid. As her esophagus expanded, I felt her tears run down my stomach and balls.

She stopped sucking and looked up at me, mascara running down her face, smiling guiltily. "I think I'm gonna barf."

"Let's go to the bathroom," I said. I peeled off my jeans and underwear, took my belt out, and placed it like a leash around her neck. I pulled on it and she followed me to the bathroom on all fours like a dog. I told her to sit by the toilet, I pushed her dress down and revealed perky, full, and smooth boobs. I twisted her pink, hardened nipples, and squeezed and slapped the meaty globes till they turned red. She instinctively made sure the dress still covered her bag, but other than that she opposed no resistance, like a perfectly trained pet.

"You shit through your nipples too?" I inquired.

She chuckled. "Not that I know of, squeeze them harder and see!"

What I did was I got down on my knees and sucked and bit those sweet nipples till they were red and raw. Then I stood up and resumed fucking her doll-face. She choked and gagged again and then puked in the toilet, yellow ropes with chunks of pizza in them. When she looked up at me, I noticed her nose was bleeding. Then she licked her blood. "I dig this. You're rougher than before."

I answered with another heavy slap that splattered some of the blood on the toilet seat. "Shut the fuck up and put your mouth to good use, you toilet whore!"

Then I resumed humping her head. I imagined her mouth was a pussy, that they surgically recreated it because cancer had claimed her vagina. All she could eat was cum, it was the only way to survive. She was paying people to fuck her and spending her time in men's rooms pointing at the dripping pussy on her face, signaling she was hungry. That fantasy made me cum deep inside her throat. Spent, I collapsed on the bathroom floor as my leg muscles were burning. Blood and saliva dripped on her chest, by her inverted cross, and between her bruised tits. We stayed there for a minute to catch our breaths.

"You feel a bit fucked in the head?" I asked with a satisfied grin.

She giggled, exposing yellowed teeth stained with blood. "I've always been fucked in the head."

As I rested, leaning against the wall, I heard a commotion

in the living room. I got up to check it out. A few books were knocked on the floor and papers were flying around haphazardly like during poltergeist activity. The gray evening light had turned dark blue. A storm was brewing. Gusts of wind came through the balcony door cooling the film of sweat on my body. I rushed to close it. Evelyn came next to me, lit up a smoke, and looked out at the incipient tempest. The strong winds flung debris from the dumpsters right outside my building into the street. The spruce trees swayed, caught in an awkward dance. A green and yellow Subway sign across the street was ripped from its frame and blown through the vacant parking lot. A woman hurried to the safety of the bus station shelter, her hair and clothes ruffled by the wind, giving her a skeletal look.

The dark gray clouds were low and suffocating. Silver lightning flashed from the blackened sky, here and there, briefly dressing different areas of the neighborhood in a dazzling, ghostly white. The rumble of thunder sounded like a celestial demolition. This reminded me of Evelyn's nightmare about the upside-down pyramid. Maybe God and his angels performed an archeological dig up in the heavens. The downpour began, rain covering the window in a myriad of streams. Darkness claimed the last remains of light and the streetlights were left to illuminate the windblown sheets of rain. A few cars drove by, their tires hissing. Two fire trucks drove toward downtown, glistening red, their sirens wailing.

I was about to make a comment like *Maybe someone got roasted* when Evelyn turned to me and gave me an open-mouthed kiss, driving her tongue deep to taste mine. She hugged me more tightly than ever before. Clinging to me. I thought the storm has triggered a sexual instinct, an atavistic drive. She tasted bad—a rancid mix of puke, salty cum, and weed—and the jagged edges of her ruined teeth scraped my tongue and lips, but I enjoyed the uninhibited intimacy.

She released me and put on one of her favorite songs, Theatre of Tragedy's "Dance of Shadows." She swayed along with the solemn, melancholy keyboard line, her fingers playing invisible claps through the air. When a harsh, doomy riff blasted, she curled her hands into fists and beat invisible drums while banging her head slowly, her eyes closed. An angelic ethereal voice filled the room and she embraced and kissed me again. My penis jolted back to life, and soon we were on the floor where I sucked on her raw tits and lifted her short dress, peeled off her lacy black underwear and stockings, and began voraciously eating her. She moaned as I inserted my fingers in her vagina and then made her lick her juices.

She whispered, "My vagina is a bit tight because of radiation. I'm like a virgin again." We both chuckled. I was stone hard and forced my way into her. She was tight but I pressed harder giving her both pleasure and pain. She started bleeding down there but said nothing. Once I settled into my groove her mangled boobs shook in the rhythm of my thrusts. Forcefully, she grabbed my right hand and placed it on her neck. I began choking her and pounding harder. She caressed the tense muscles of my forearm. The heavenly voice sang:

> *I am so alone;*
> *Eternal loneliness—*
> *Thoughts only for me,*
> *I whisper with the shadow—*
> *I dance with the shadow—*
> *I go about alone,*
> *I want the blood: Dance of Death.*
> *Dance no more with the shadow,*
> *Please do not dance across the grave;*
> *Dance with me Lucifer's waltz.*
> *I long to be your bride*

To become darkness.

Her wide-open eyes fixed on the ceiling. Her left hand went under her black dress and she ripped the colostomy bag and played with her stoma as if it were a clit. Pasty shit oozed from the hole. I averted my eyes. The sight and the stench were not particularly erotic. I continued choking and pounding her and soon her body tensed, jolted by a massive orgasm. As her juices lubricated my cock, her vagina gently squeezed my penis like a loving hand. I pressed harder on her throat and she continued caressing my arm.

> *Embrace me, till I die,*
> *And I shall resurrect (again)...*
> *I love you.*

Her face was red, and her eyes bulged looking at the ceiling, strangely detached, like she tried to remember or imagine something. Windpipe almost crushed, her tongue protruded from her mouth as tortured choking sounds came from deep inside her throat. She didn't tap out, which was our signal when kinky sex became too painful.

I knew she wouldn't tap out as she wanted to die, no doubt about it.

I had known it since she had winked at me back at the bookstore. She needed my help to reach the exit. Her right hand kept fingering her stoma, dress getting increasingly soiled and shit staining my carpet. She orgasmed one more time and then her body relaxed, her fingers moving more slowly and then stopping. Soon after I managed to finish inside her and then pulled out. I kept choking her with all my might till her face turned blue and her eyes glazed over. The white of the eyes was spotted with blood as if the last thing she saw has pushed needles into her eyeballs.

I leaned back against the couch, wheezing, struggling to catch my breath. I settled down after a few minutes and wiped away the sweat dripping in my eyes. I couldn't believe I killed her. This was my first kill, and I felt exhilarated by the rush of adrenaline and the full presence of death. I beamed with pride because I stuck to my nihilistic principles and didn't try to "save" Evelyn. I just decreased the universal mass of trembling flesh by about one hundred and fifty pounds. Had Schopenhauer killed anyone? Had Cioran put anyone out of their misery with his bare hands? Not likely. Though it was worth nothing, I was the new champion of pessimism. The victories of the nihilist are always bitter. My ego aside, I truly felt like I helped, that I did an act of kindness out of love. And I was flattered she chose me. She knew I'd understand. "Thank you," I said to her. "I set you free." Then a line from Cioran popped in my head. "I long to be free—desperately free. Free as the stillborn are free." With her short hair, she had a babyface, a gloomy baby. If strangled by the umbilical cord in her mother's womb all of this mess could have been avoided.

Slowly my adrenaline dropped, and I felt all my muscles hurt. Her body looked eerie and disgusting. She was now a damaged Goth Barbie, broken and forgotten by a mentally ill girl, ready for an eternity of gathering dust in a box down in the basement. I couldn't believe that I was talking to her one hour ago and enjoying her spirit and personality. Now, she was but an inconvenience, a foreign object that perturbed my room's order, garbage in need of disposal. I considered going to bed and forgetting about it, but I was afraid she would start smelling worse once decomposition set in. The room already reeked of shit and pot. I staggered to my bedroom, fetched the bottle of Febreze, and sprayed in a wide arc above the dead body.

I plopped on the couch and turned off the music. I

needed to focus on the problem at hand. I couldn't get rid of the body during the day tomorrow, in broad daylight. Although I knew what I did was right, I was confident the police wouldn't see things my way. They were just as prejudiced as doctors, institutionalized people with no understanding of metaphysical issues like the meaning of life.

I have to clean up my mess, I thought, standing up.

I turned off the lights to cover my actions, got dressed again, and went out on the balcony. Wind-driven rain hit my face like icy needles. I was on the second floor. Two dumpsters were under my balcony. I leaned over the railing and saw no lights coming from the apartment below. All other windows were dark as well. Across the street past the strip mall was a residential area. Trees obscured their view of my building. No lights glimmered either. The rain seemed to have lulled everyone to sleep.

I went back and lifted her in my arms, she was heavy. Crossing on the balcony I thought I looked like a groom taking his wife inside their new home. Except I was taking her out into the rainy night, to her garbage-filled tomb. I rested her body on the railing and with my final ounces of energy flung her over.

She fell on the full bags of trash with a muffled thud, a dark equivalent of a kid jumping in a ball pit. I took some of my garbage and placed her colostomy bag in it. I put on my jeans, shoes, and black hoodie, and I went downstairs to make sure her body was adequately hidden. The gusting wind slammed the door shut behind me, making the glass tremble. I tied up my hoodie strings. Rounding the corner I squinted my eyes against the downpour and checked again the lights on this side of the building. All windows were dark. Gazing inside the dumpster I saw her pale face shimmering with rain in the pale glare of the streetlights. Bloodshot eyes stared up at the black sky—a martyr with no faith. She seemed to be resting peacefully in her bed of trash, surrounded by wet black plastic bags rippling in the wind. A white empty plastic egg carton, a broken-down Ikea chair, and a battered pair of Nikes further adorned her tomb. I covered her head and torso with my bags and spread the existing ones over the rest of her body. Sometimes homeless people came to poke around for goodies but this night was too stormy and even those poor souls must have been resting.

Back by the entrance, I lit up a smoke as distant lightning flashed. To me, thunderstorms were God having panic attacks, and the rain was the sweat of his fear. In an inversion of roles, his lightning was his prayer to his creation, but there was no Moses with his tablets at the receiving end; the blast was a random neural flare choked by the spider webs of a demented brain. Both man and God have forgotten their covenant and were caught in an entropic whirlwind of anger and senility.

My attention drifted from the gloomy vision and I noticed Evelyn's red VW Beetle in the guest parking lot. The keys must have been in her bag upstairs. I'd have to drive it to a different side of the city tomorrow. I knew I took many risks and did a terrible job covering my crime. I was betting on the garbage truck coming before some random low-life would poke through the trash. *Tomorrow is Monday*, I thought, feeling that the truck should come on Mondays. Also, I was betting on neighbors not noticing the car overnight. At least her folks were in BC and it would be a while till she was reported missing.

Unfortunately for me, people saw us together at the bookstore and she posted on Facebook she planned on attending the event. I was the last person she was seen with. If the police came to my place, that would be the end. First, I sucked at lying and even a rookie would find me suspicious. Second, her fingerprints and DNA were everywhere and I knew I wouldn't bother cleaning it. Plus, if they found the body, my semen was inside her, which would be an easy match. It was a matter of time till they caught me. I was a dead man walking.

But this wasn't a new thing for me. The current circumstances injected a bit of anxiety and urgency into my long-held belief that I was but a walking meatbag. Plus, jail wasn't for me. The prison of the world made me claustrophobic enough as it was. So, all in all, this was an excellent opportunity to use my insurance policy. Murder-suicide or suicide by cop? I had to think about it. Then another thought struck me. Evelyn knew I was reckless and lazy and would do an awful job covering the crime. So, maybe, in her way, she was repaying my gift post-mortem by having a cop punch my ticket to freedom.

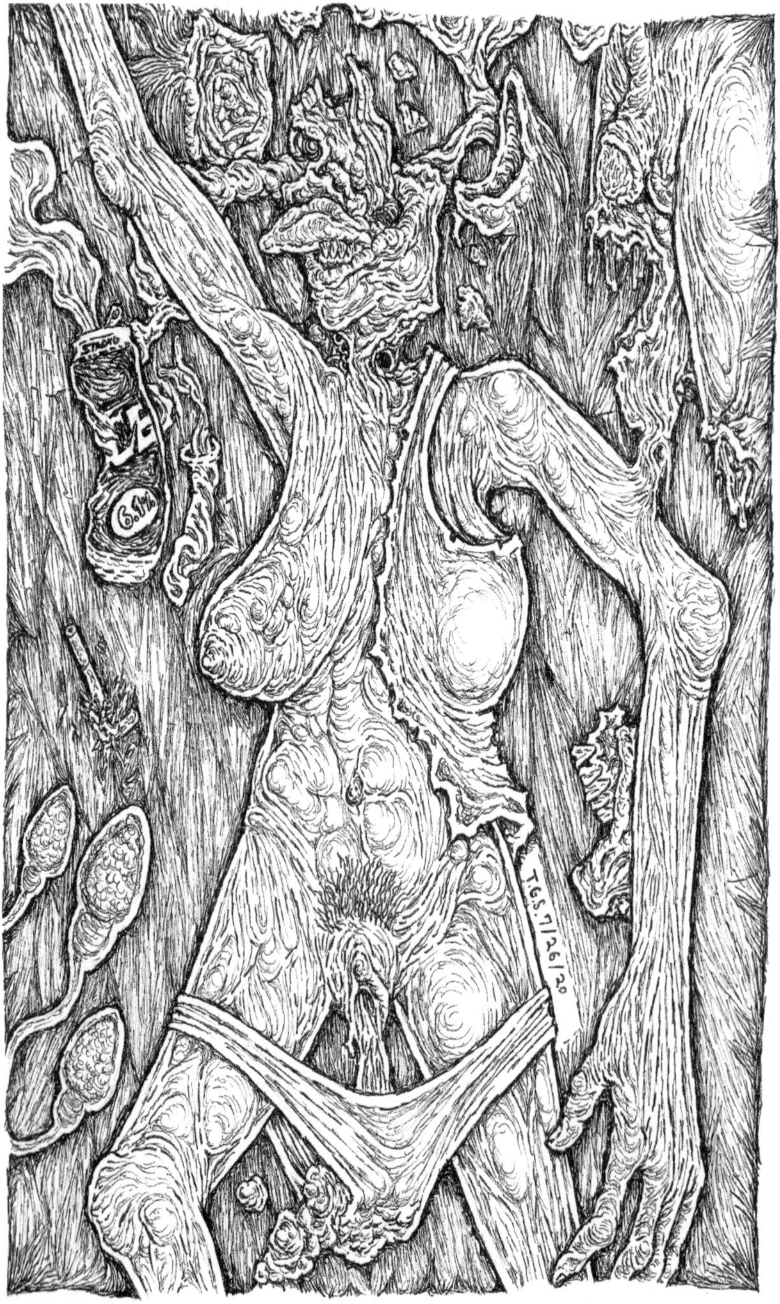
6.9%
T.G.S. 7/26/20

DEAD SEED

"Come on, stand up and walk," I prodded Will, like a priest during a spiritual healing ceremony.

"I'll be fine once I have my coffee, junior," he said, avoiding my gaze and sinking deeper into the couch. I doubted coffee had anything to do with his condition. I was puzzled as he had all the symptoms of a stroke—vision and balance problems. But, they had developed gradually since Christmas. When I had sent him on an errand to City Center Mall, he had knocked over a Christmas tree by mistake, causing an argument with security. The other day, he had slipped on the ice while shoveling snow for Becky and got an ugly bruise on the side of his face. Plus, countless times, he had bumped into doors or walls around the house like a defective robot.

"Come on, man, stand up!" I pleaded again, offering my right hand for support. He looked at me with bloodshot blue eyes clouded by drinking and insomnia, trying to gauge how serious I was. He grabbed my arm with a shaky, bony hand and stood up for a bit, his legs apart like a toddler processing his first step, then plopped onto the couch again. It was like his brain impulses were hitting a wall of stubborn muscles. Will started crying, "I don't know what's happening to me," he blubbered. His white dog Princess felt his pain and came and sat by his useless legs.

"Okay, we have to go to the emergency. I'm calling Moe," I said and pressed the landlord's name on my phone. Moe was familiar with Will's medical history and also worked for The University of Alberta Hospital. "Hey Moe, it's Jeremy. Will took a turn. He can't walk...No, he doesn't want to talk, he's in denial, and doesn't want people fussing over him. Can you give us a ride, please?" He said he'd come in ten minutes. Conversation over, I sat down on the couch next to Will.

"Moe asked if I knew CPR," I told Will and rubbed his skinny thigh.

Will smacked my hand. "Don't touch me, Germy. Just let me die in peace!" My name is Jeremy, but Will would call me Germy on account of my iffy hygiene habits. I don't know about you, but showering makes me depressed. I've always preferred the protection of a few layers of sweat.

"But I want to tongue your toothless mouth," I said and stuck my tongue out.

Will recoiled in disgust. "Princess, keep Booger King away from Daddy, okay?" The fat and ratty-looking dog perked her ears when hearing her name and looked at me placidly with her eyes of different colors, one hazel and the other blue.

"This dog is fat *and* stupid," I said, heading upstairs to my bedroom.

"Don't call her that. You're gonna give her a complex," Will shouted.

In my room, I put on my jeans and placed my *Walking Dead* graphic novel in my backpack. Back downstairs, I donned my black hoodie, stepped into my Columbia winter shoes, and then helped Will put on his Sperry shoes and worn-out winter jacket. The only winter footwear he had were his Kamik boots, but those weren't needed for a trip to the hospital.

Soon, out of the bay window, we saw Moe's gray minivan park in front of the house, close to a gap in the bank of snow lining the street. Originally from Egypt, Moe was a tall, middle-aged man with a long gentle face. Grabbing Will by the shoulders, we helped him walk, his feet trudging through the snow slowly. Crushed by the unbearable humiliation, Will started crying again, and Moe assured him that everything would be okay in his gentle and calm voice. Moe claimed the wait wouldn't be long given Will's medical history, especially the lung cancer he had fought last year.

One of the nurses gave Will a wheelchair when he went through triage. Moe spread more encouragement and positive vibes, told us to message him with the news, and went back to work. Despite Moe's reassurances, we ended up waiting a few hours.

I read my novel and looked around from time to time. Nearby, an old woman sat on her walker and stared at me. She looked ancient: wispy white hair barely covering her scalp, translucent skin stretched over brittle bones, a face frozen in a rictus, and gray eyes trapping a faded awareness. Why didn't she kill herself? What kept her going? This made me wonder: what was the difference between this woman and a zombie? Granted, she wasn't aggressive or a cannibal—she could only probably ingest soft foods. Mentally she had the same effect on the living, radiating the same hypnotic soul-sucking grayness a hoard of zombies would.

This made me consider the origins of this zombie notion. Medical science had become so advanced that elderly people just wouldn't die. It was unnatural. They stuck around like skeletal reminders of our own mortality, with the sole perverse purpose of bringing the healthy populace to psychological ruin. Their moaning was subliminal, and it'd invade your subconscious like a nest of earworms, till one day you found yourself eating a bullet for no apparent reason, your splattered brains on the wall crawling with big, fat maggots.

These morbid thoughts were making me depressed, a thick fog clouding my brain. I felt I was melting as if some demon removed all bones from my body, and my flesh liquefied like wax. I realized I forgot to take my meds and quickly reached for the backpack and breathed a sigh of relief when my fingers touched the bottles of Prozac and Ativan in the front pocket. I popped my pills quickly. I tried to cheer myself up and see if there were no cutie-pies in the emergency room—no such luck. Even the nurses looked beaten with the ugly stick. Right then, one called Will's name, and I pushed his wheelchair out of the first limbo.

A nurse took us to a hospital bed, closed the blue curtains around it, and gave Will a white gown. She said the doctor will be with us in a second. I helped Will dress and then sat on a chair as he lay in bed. Finally, the doctor came in. He was young, blond, and well-built, with intelligent blue eyes.

He looked at Will and asked bluntly, "Who beat you up? Look, you have bruises all over your hands and face."

Indeed, the short-sleeved hospital gown revealed Will's battered arms. Caught with his guard down, Will went quiet, and I had to explain he had fallen on the ice while shoveling snow.

"Have you been drinking, Will?" the doctor asked. This second question made Will more ashamed and confused, his mouth agape.

I jumped again to his defense. "These symptoms aren't from drinking, he developed balance and vision problems over the last two months, and it got worse and worse. It has nothing to do with drinking."

"All right," the doctor said, "let's do some exercises. Will, can you stand up for me, please?"

Will managed to stand but failed the tests miserably, often mistaking left for right and vice-versa and misunderstanding the doctor's instructions. He'd laugh at times and say he wasn't drunk, just sick. The doctor ordered a CT scan, and a nurse took Will away in his wheelchair. When he returned to the room, another nurse came to check his vitals.

"We have *WWE* tonight?" Will asked me.

"No, it's *Ice Road Truckers*, I think. They keep changing the time for wrestling. Roman Reigns will fight Brock Lesner at Wrestlemania, though."

"Oh boy, that will be something to watch."

After about half an hour of arguing who's gonna win the Heavyweight Championship, the doctor finally came back, sat on a chair, got close to Will, and said, "Will, I'm afraid I have some bad news. There's a black mass in your brain, most likely a tumor. In all probability, your lung cancer has metastasized. The tumor is pressing on your cerebellum and occipital lobe, which is what gave rise to the vision and balance problems you were rightly concerned about. I know this is a lot to take in, but I assure you there are some good treatment options on the table."

Throughout this, I had the surreal sense I was in a soap opera. I didn't know exactly what I had expected, but this was brutal. The news pulverized Will. It happened all around me. Something in the room broke, like a psychic earthquake, as if he exhaled his ectoplasmic soul, which was then savagely ripped to shreds. I actually felt exhilarated; I felt the true, chaotic nature of the universe reveal itself at that moment. The dark chaos mercilessly ripped through what Will called "reality" and shouted, *You're nothing! The cosmos doesn't give a shit about you!*

All Will could manage through hot tears was, "I just want to see Princess, my baby dog."

I had to call Moe and Will's friend Becky with the bad

news. I told Becky Will wouldn't be able to shovel the snow for her anymore on account of a newly discovered brain tumor. She sounded concerned and said she'd stop by the house later. Moe came and gave us a ride back and reminded Will that we have one of the greatest cancer treatment centers in the world.

Once back home, Will smoked and cried and cried and smoked some more. I told him that maybe radiation would work, but I didn't believe it myself. He was dead meat and not even that much meat. I read somewhere that brain tumors sometimes grow hairs and teeth. This reminded me of Stephen King's *The Dark Half*, the brother who gets sucked while in the embryo and survives only as a milky eye and a set of teeth in his stronger twin's brain. I thought that when Will fell into his shallow sleep, those teeth moved and formed words: *I got you now, Willy-boy. Gonna take you with me six feet under, and we're gonna eat dirt for all eternity. Eat dirt, and smoke, and cry.*

But you should never underestimate the survival instinct. It may disappear for a day or two but then it comes back in full force, in a different, more seductive form. Soon, Will started buying my bullshit about the wonders of chemo and radiation. "Oh yeah, they have the best Cancer Treatment Center here in Edmonton," he'd repeat his new mantra. "I'm in good hands. The doctors here are the best in the world, Becky and Moe told me." The dark truths Will chose to avoid were that his cancer could spread further to other organs or his bones and that maybe his original lung cancer hadn't been completely removed.

As winter turned to spring, Will was hospitalized and did an entire course of radiation therapy. He was back home in time for the playoffs, and, as the Edmonton Oilers were playing well, the old man was as happy as can be, trying to forget about the tumor (if it was still there) by whipping his nervous system with alcohol and nicotine. I was more than happy to join.

☣

We were watching *WWE* and working on a fifteen-pack of Black Ice when the doorbell rang, and Princess started barking. Tail up in the air, she jumped up and down as if she'd charge but then turned her head to me for assistance.

"She's a guard dog this one," Will joked.

Groaning, I got up from my armchair and went to the door. Becky's smiling face was framed by the door's window. Her black hair was cut short, manly, and she had intense blue eyes, a bit clouded over by age and meds. In my experience, most women over fifty struggled with depression, so I assumed it was meds.

I opened the door and invited her in. She handed me a full bag, "Hey Jeremy, I got some food for you and Will."

"Oh, thank you," I said and caught a glimpse down the cleavage of her black top as she removed her shoes. She still sported a nice rack, even if a bit saggy.

"There's the patient!" Becky exclaimed, seeing Will through the living room's French doors. "I got you some homemade chicken soup, Will. How are you holding up?"

"Not too bad, Becky. Come on in!"

Becky said, "Jeremy, can you put the soup in the fridge? There's some dessert too. Help yourself." Then she stepped into the living room.

I took the bag to the kitchen. There was a plastic container full of brownies. I could have eaten them all but decided to put only half a dozen on a plate. Back in my armchair, I scarfed down three brownies, chasing them with a big gulp of beer, and belched loudly. Down by my feet, Princess was mooching, licking her snout.

"Don't give her any, Jeremy. Chocolate ain't good for dogs," Will said.

"I wasn't planning on it," I said, smiling. Then I turned my attention back to *WWE* but couldn't help but hear Will and Becky talking.

"I'm feeling not too bad but am very tired," Will said. "These Ensure protein bottles are good, though, as I have no appetite." There were many Ensure bottles on the coffee table, but I bet Will was a bit ashamed by the empty beer cans next to them.

"Don't worry, Will. You'll love my chicken soup. It will invigorate your body and soothe your soul."

Next, Paige, the *WWE* Diva Champion, came on big screen TV, and I got lost in her sensual movements and tuned out the conversation between Becky and Will. Did the pale Goth-looking British bombshell shave her pussy, or did she sport a small tuft of dark hair over her glistening sex? Was it a triangle or more of a narrow rectangle? Her ass was a bit flat yet still inviting. I made a mental note to check for her nudes on the internet.

Becky words woke me from my erotic daydream like a drilling machine. She said, "I think God has blessed you, Will. He gave you the gift of time. You should be grateful for each and every day. You should come to Church with my husband and me, and we can pray together."

I turned to her and said, "Was his cancer a gift from God too?"

Becky gazed at me, slightly annoyed by the interruption but still wearing a forgiving plastic smile. "God works in mysterious ways, sometimes he puts us on trial—"

"Is that so?" I asked, interrupting her nonsense. "What if Will's tumor grew so big it gave him a stroke and left him paralyzed or landed him in a coma? What would he have to learn from that, since, you know, comatose brains aren't known for their learning abilities?" I rubbed my chin and made a *hmmm* sound. Then I said, "And is being in a coma the gift of time as well? If so, I'd gladly return it."

Becky's face turned from slight discomfort to burning hatred. "That's blasphemy, young man. You're taking God's name in vain. You can't give back what God offered you!"

I straightened up in my armchair as if electrocuted. "Then how is it a gift if you can't return or re-gift? Or is it more like a curse? I'd happily blow my brains out before unwrapping those wonderful gifts."

"I feel sorry for your lost soul. There's a special place in Hell for suicides."

"That's right, the fabled human soul, what neuroscientists from universities around the globe have been struggling to find for the last century? That one?" Becky took a breath, getting ready to answer, but I stuck my right hand up. "Shush, cretin! It was a rhetorical question! Anyway, let me get this straight: if I don't take his shitty gifts, your God will torture me forever? He sounds like a high school bully in desperate need of therapy. Was he abused as a child?"

Now her eyes were bulging with rage. "Just because *you* sold your soul to the Devil doesn't mean others don't have one."

"Oh yeah?" I said, stood up abruptly, and rushed toward her. In the corner of my eye, I saw Will's eyes widen and Princess sitting up, perking her ears, ready to bolt. Becky flinched, thinking I'm going to strike her. I yelled in her face, "And where is your soul exactly, somewhere between your saggy boobs and your dried-up pussy, you menopausal freak? Or right behind those narcotized blind eyes? Can I peek through those grimy windows? Should I bring a magnifying glass?"

"Jeremy, enough of this!" Will shouted and smashed his fist on the coffee table. A few bottles fell on the floor, and

Princess ran from the room, tail between her legs. "You're stressing me out, boy! I'm a sick man. I can't deal with this shit. You have to show some respect to my guest and be nice, don't be yourself for once."

I looked at him, eyes burning with tears of frustration, strangled by the torrent of insults I needed to vomit on that spreader of Christian disease. "Okay, one more thing," I said, raising my index finger. "What you have to do, Becky, is put your God on a leash and bring him here to Will," I pointed my finger to the floor area in front of Will, "and have him pray for Will's forgiveness. Okay? Until then, shut your stupid trap!"

I stormed out of the room, banging the French doors shut. The sound of window panes smashing on the floor in my wake was gratifying. I blasted death metal on loud in my bedroom and drew a lion fucking Becky from behind. Her arms were torn off, lying on the sides of her body, right hand still clutching a crucifix. Claws ripped her back to shreds and her face contorted in agony. I wrote the caption with a smile, "Lion Fucking Dumpster Haunted by Jesus."

☣

By the first intermission, the Oilers had the lead against the Red Wings and looked poised to win the playoff series. Will and I went out on the front stairs for a smoke. The sledgehammer Will had used to work on our front picket fence last summer rested against one of the porch walls, next to an old pair of work boots a tenant had left behind.

"No one stole the sledgehammer or boots," I said, "and we never lock this porch door."

"Are you thick between the ears, boy? Thieves don't like to work."

"You're as dumb as you're ugly. You can split someone's

head with that shit. It can build your tough guy rep in the hood."

Will took a drag and shook his head. "It's too heavy to carry, numbskull. These Injuns are so fucked-up on drugs they can barely walk."

I let the matter drop and lit up my smoke. The retreating snow uncovered the grass from last year, and all the cigarette butts we had flicked around during winter. Here and there, clumps of bright green fought against the desolate brown. I had a long-sleeved black shirt, but Will wore his gray winter jacket and black tuque. Although there was only a mild breeze in the air, he was more sensitive to cold on account of his blood thinners.

As if to illustrate Will's point, a drunk Native guy stumbled through the puddles on the sidewalk heading toward 109th. Sleazy dark hair covered his brown, puffed-up face. His gait tilted a bit to the right. He wore a black hoodie proclaiming "You're on Native Land", battered boots, and lowered jeans, barely holding on to his emaciated frame.

"Is it five o'clock yet?" I joked and squinted at Will through the cigarette smoke.

"I think I know him; I remember his hoodie," Will said. "One morning, I was smoking here, and he asked to bum one. Then he asked me if it was morning or night."

We both laughed.

"These Injuns smoke too much whaky tobaky if you ask me," Will said.

"Yeah, and drink like fish. Didn't they rob that liqueur store by Safeway a week ago or so?"

"Yup, on a Saturday night to boot. Tied up the poor employees in the freezer, for God's sake. Now they have a security guy there all the time."

"Damn," I said and took a drag. Then I asked, "Do you

wanna go for drinks on Whyte if the Oilers win? It's gonna be wild. It's the weekend too."

"Nah, I'm too old for that sort of thing. I'll just finish the pack and sleep next to Princess, the love of my life. If I can get any sleep."

"Fuck," I sighed. "That's okay, you're too ugly anyway...and fucking old. You'd just cramp my style."

"You have a style?" Will jested. "What's that? The creep who casually gets too close to a woman in a crowd. Then he cops a feel while fondling himself in his pants?"

I forced out a laugh but felt dead inside. The ugly truth was I had no one to go for drinks with. Born and raised in this shithole of a town and no friends to show for it, except a terminal cancer patient. Even my parents seemed to avoid me. They had moved from Edmonton to British Columbia and told me at the last moment. *Subtext: you're a useless slob, and we'll pretend you don't exist.*

"Well, at least my junk still works," I said, trying to keep the dark thoughts at bay.

"Yeah? And what good is that?" Will gave me a brown grin.

"Not much, sadly. It's been a long drought."

"I know, junior. I bet your right hand is all soft and creamy from too much Vaseline."

"Oh yeah, I bet I can get a rise out of you with my creamy hand," I said and made to grab his crotch.

Will stepped away laughing. "Don't touch me, you perv. Princess, *sic*!" Will pointed at me, but the dog just fetched a stick off the ground and wagged her tail.

"Seriously though, you should go, spud. People party all over Whyte, beer is flowing, girls show off their boobs. Who knows, you might get lucky. Stranger things have happened. Maybe you can land a drunk fatty, more cushin' for the pushin'. But you have to be sober enough to find the wet spot."

Will's last words were almost drowned by the sirens of two ambulances rushing toward 109th. We gazed at them placidly.

"Maybe it would be easier to just buy an escort and go without food for a week or two," I mused.

"Nah, I don't see you going without food. Let's face it, Jeremy, you're a fucking pig. After a day without food, you'd barbecue Princess here. I know you. But I bet you could find some cheap crack whores downtown, on 118st. Any port in a storm, eh?"

I looked at him through a haze of smoke, "118st? That sounds pretty far. Do they have any mentally ill ones in the bunch? I figure you don't even have to pay those cause they don't know any better. You can build a nice cage for her in the basement. It will give you something to do. Hell, we can even train her to clean the house...with her tongue." I tilted my head back and laughed hysterically, slapping my knee.

Will smiled and shook his head. "Boy, you're one sick puppy. They should have put you down from the get-go."

"It's true, I is severely handicapped, sir. I have papers from the guv'mint to prove it, dear sir. Can I give you hand-job for five dollars? Doctor says cum good." I contorted my face and let a string of saliva escape the corner of my mouth.

Will bent over laughing when the drunk Native appeared again at the corner of the yard. He seemed to want to climb over the small, white picket fence, but his movements were too uncoordinated, and he fell on his face in the muddy grass. Will and I started laughing even harder. The drunk got back to his feet and gave us a wild look. Mud and blades of grass stuck on his bloated face and in his hair, a feral grumble escaping his throat. His eyes rolled deep in his head, giving him a savage appearance. For a split second, I thought he was either blind or wearing blind eye contacts like in horrors. But he seemed too out of it to be playing a prank. He looked genuinely sick.

Princess started barking, and the drunk stumbled toward her. Will walked up to him and shouted, "Hey, stop right there! What do you think you're doing here?" The junkie outstretched his hands and lurched at Will. More out of surprise, Will fell on his back and raised his right hand to protect his face. The drunk bit into the cloth-covered forearm.

I sprang to my feet and punched the attacker in the head, repeatedly, with all my might. Blood oozed from his mangled ear. The Native kept his jaws clenched around Will's hand like a pitbull. His hands scratched at Will's face and pulled down his tuque over his eyes, blinding him.

Princess was barking and biting the attacker's leg. In a flash, I remembered the sledgehammer. I ran up the stairs, banged the porch door open, and grabbed the tool. Back on the lawn, I raised it and hit the back of the freakish intruder. I heard the wet thud of injured flesh and the crack of broken bones. The attacker didn't let go, but his movements slowed.

The second strike aimed for his head. I held back a bit, afraid to hit Will, but the hammer still had enough power to crack the drunk's skull. Bright blood oozed from greasy black hair. His body went limp. Will pushed him away like a stinky blanket and struggled to his feet, gasping for breath. He adjusted his tuque and looked around wild-eyed.

"What the fuck was that?"

I caught my breath and said, "He was probably on some heavy fucking drugs, possibly PCP. I saw a documentary about that shit. Look at his eyes. They're all white. Were they white when he asked you for a smoke?"

Will shook his head and frowned at the dead body now sprawled on our lawn.

STILLBORN GALLERY

I crouched next to the corpse and pressed on his eyeballs to see if he was wearing lenses. The globes were milky white, and blood began to ooze from their edges as I kept on rubbing them. I asked, "Should we call 911?"

Then we heard fireworks coming from Safeway. But it was a Saturday afternoon. They must have been gunshots. Will said, "Junior, we better get inside and turn on the local news. There's something wrong with this picture."

☣

We didn't have to turn on the local news. Edmonton was already making national news. While we were outside fighting the junkie, breaking news interrupted our hockey game. What they reported was incredible. It was on CBC, and Peter Mansbridge was all serious and gloomy about it, shaken to the core, so we figured it must be true.

Canada, and Alberta in specific, was under attack by Saudi terrorists. It was chemical and biological warfare. They poisoned the water supplies of all of central and northern Alberta. "If you live in those areas, do not drink tap water!" the reporter advised. The contaminated water turned you into what appeared to be zombies, violent flesh-eating creatures that won't die unless shot in the head. Noise mainly attracted them.

The Saudis' goal was to shut down the oil production in Northern Alberta, thus bumping up the price of their own "unethical" oil. The anchorman said, "The police advise all Albertans to barricade in their homes or places of work and avoid all contact with the infected. The Prime Minister is holding an emergency meeting with the heads of the Canadian Military Forces to decide on a response to this brutal terrorist attack."

Disturbing footage followed with a red news ticker

warning "Alberta Under Terrorist Attack" and Mansbridge's mournful commentary in the background. The hockey arena was now a bloodbath, spectators stampeding for the exits, hockey players fighting the infected and cutting their necks and faces with their blades, frenzied zombies tearing into jugulars, fountains of blood splattering on the white ice.

There was aerial footage of the High Level Bridge from one of the news helicopters. At first, it looked like protesters blocking traffic, but it was the zombie hoards congesting the street. Traffic jams clogged the roadways, and a fire spilled smoke in the clear blue sky. Then we witnessed panicked people jumping off the bridge into the gray water below. I felt the same panic I had when watching the 9/11 attacks, except this time it was amplified by the fact that the shocking images on TV, the carnage and mayhem, took place, literally and figuratively, in our very backyard.

Will and I glanced at each other wide-eyed and then gazed at the coffee table overflowing with empty beer cans. Neither of us had drunk water in days. Then we looked outside, eyes filled with terror and confusion as if the air itself were contaminated. My tormented psyche kept screaming, *This can't be real.* I felt close to zoning out.

"Camel humpers," Will muttered. "I bet our government will turn around and nuke them straight to Allah."

"Oh God, I hate them brownies so much," I said in agreement, getting a tentative grip on the situation. "I wonder if the US is gonna be on the side of Canada, as they import oil from the fuckin' Saudis too."

"But they import tons of other stuff from us, let alone oil. Our trade with them is in the billions, sonny!"

Before I could reply, I realized we headed into a political discussion when more concrete action was needed. I was able to channel my fight or flight response in a positive direction. Will didn't know as much about zombies as I did. When it came to the undead, I'd read enough books, saw enough movies, and played enough games to know the main goal was *survival*. I asked, "Do you have any more full water jugs from Safeway?"

Will rubbed his stubble. "Only one, I think."

"Fuck, we need to run to Safeway, man. We can't live on this shitty beer for long. A jug of water only buys us a day or two." I knew, when it came to survival, water was more important than food. Without water, you were dead in a week.

Right then, as if to confirm the news and give us a sense of urgency, an ambulance and two police cruisers drove past our house at high speed, their sirens wailing. Then we heard more gunshots.

Suddenly, I felt electrified. The presence of death always excited me. I was the type to laugh at a funeral. I was up and ready to go when Will said, "Hold your horses, junior! We need to go prepared. It will probably be busy, and sounds like bullets are already flying." The old man stumbled down to the basement and came back with two Glocks. I knew he had guns down there. Will was, deep down, a redneck who thought Alberta was the Canadian counterpart of Texas. He gave me a loaded handgun—fifteen rounds—and said it was ready to go.

The weapon felt good in my hand. It instantly gave me a sense of power. Will grabbed the other Glock and stuffed it in his waistband. I decided to run to my bedroom upstairs and grab my black hoodie and backpack. I placed the gun in the big front pocket of the hoodie.

Armed with the handguns, we left the house and walked to the grocery store. The sight of the Safeway parking lot and entrance gave us pause. Pure pandemonium. It seemed in half an hour, all civilization collapsed. The world had turned into pure anarchy. My excitement skyrocketed.

A few hundred people struggled to enter the store as others tried to get out with their loot. For a second, this reminded me of the crowds you see outside malls on Black Friday or Boxing Day—except for the broken windows, the gunshots, and the zombies. Someone smashed one of the big windows with a cart, and others did the same in quick succession. Then people jumped into the store, some cutting themselves on the jagged remains of the glass. You could tell the undead by their shuffling gaits, their slack, expressionless faces, and how they didn't carry anything, no bags or baskets. Their food was all around in huge supply—living flesh.

The bulk of the zombie hoard came from Whyte. Circling the grocery store, more dead shuffled from 109th. In the maelstrom, I recognized Sue, one of the cashiers. She chomped a customer's jugular, blood splattering on her face and work uniform. A policeman shot her in the back, and she turned to him. The second bullet went through one of her milky eyes and out the back of her head. She dropped to the ground but then another undead, built like a football linebacker, blindsided the shooter, and ripped the skin off his right cheek. The policeman uttered a piercing scream and elbowed the zombie. The corpse had a stronghold of his neck, and he chokeslammed the officer, breaking his skull on the pavement, and then proceeded to savagely feed on the victim's brains.

Cars, some already involved in collisions, steam rising from their hoods, filled the congested parking lot. The ones driving away cut through the green areas surrounding the store and the parking lot and then joined the already chaotic traffic on Whyte. The looters scurrying away with filled carts were probably from our neighborhood.

I knew instinctively that if we joined the chaos, we'd die. Part of me wanted to do it anyway. I was deliberating when I saw Becky and her husband pushing carts filled with jugs of water and canned food. I recognized her short, *I-want-to-*

speak-to-your-manager haircut, and her determined gait. Her husband, chubby and balding, sporting a pair of thick black-rimmed glasses, walked behind his wife. They were in a rush to get home, looking down and frowning, shook by the ungodly bedlam.

"Let's shoot them and take their stuff," I said matter-of-factly.

Will looked at me with incredulous eyes, still struggling to process the chaotic developments.

"Man, we're not gonna survive in there, let alone manage to grab anything. This is the Wild West now, the law of the jungle," I explained, pointing at the carnage.

"But Becky is a good friend. She's Christian. She'll help us," Will managed in an uncertain tone.

"Okay, ask her for a jug of water then," I said in frustration, thinking, *You can't teach an old dog new tricks*.

Becky and her husband pushed the full, clamoring carts across the street, looking nervously left and right. Will and I were on the sidewalk, right by their house. Once they crossed the street, they kept their heads low, pretending not to see us.

"Hi Becky," Will called. "Looks like the Apocalypse is upon us, Jesus Murphy!" He forced laughter. "You think you can please help us with one of those jugs of water. We only have one left. We'll be dead within a week."

Becky stopped and looked at us like we were strangers. "Go get your own," she barked and pointed to the besieged grocery store.

I moved strategically in front of their carts and said, "That would be a death sentence. Plus, they're probably out of water by now."

"And how's that my problem...*Germy*?" she spitted, looking at me like I was a cockroach. Her using that nickname made me grab the handle of my gun tighter in my pocket. I only allowed Will to call me that.

Will, sensing the building tension, said, "Becky, we're just asking as a neighbor for some water. Isn't that the Christian thing to do, love and help thy neighbor?"

"This is an emergency Will, and God helps those who help themselves," Becky's husband retorted in a soft, effeminate voice that made clear who wore the pants in that marriage.

I said, "Oh, so the Christian love you preach doesn't apply in emergency situations?"

Becky's husband's narcotized eyes bulged with hate behind his thick glasses, but no reply came.

Becky ran her hand nervously through her hair and turned to Will. "Let's face it, my friend, you're terminal, don't have much left. You should be grateful for the few more months God gave you and go home and pray for him to have mercy on your soul, as you have many sins to atone for from what I heard. As for this disgusting onanist creep who does nothing but eats and masturb—"

My bullet cut Becky's rant short. It pierced her forehead, freezing the puzzlement on her face, and exited the back of the skull in a spray of blood, bits of bone, and brains. Some of it splattered the husband's face, painting one of his glasses' lenses red. I inhaled acrid gunpowder. Becky fell on the ground, her blood pooling on the gray sidewalk. Her husband looked at me, wild-eyed, shouting something I couldn't make out as my ears buzzed from the blast. My wrist hurt from shooting the gun one-handed, and I took a step back, pointed the weapon at the husband, supported it with my left hand, and squeezed the trigger again. The bullet punched his head back. He swayed on his feet for a second like a drunk and then crumbled next to his beloved.

"Take that Christian scum!" I shouted as a red curtain of blind rage fell over my eyesight, adrenaline pumping in my veins. I saw myself stepping toward Becky and kicking and stomping on her head, frenzied by the sound of her skull breaking against the concrete. When I was done, her head was a bloody pulp devoid of any human features, one of her eyeballs lying in the grassy area by the street, like a lost golf ball.

In hindsight, I think what triggered me—pun intended—was that Becky proved to be a bully. Under the loving Christian mask, she was full of resentment. I had been the butt of cruel jokes since middle school when the other students started calling me *Germy* instead of Jeremy. I had the nervous habit of picking my nose, but I never ate my boogers. However, most kids claimed I did, solidifying my cruel nickname.

Also, as I already mentioned, my personal hygiene had always been iffy. I was already pretty big by then, and while no one tried to physically bully me, they did it mentally. Every time I tried to talk to another classmate, they would mockingly pick their noses, laugh, and run away. Harsh jokes like that get to you when you're a kid. I withdrew and ate junk food and sweets, played video games. Soon I became Booger King. Slowly, a kind of curtain of invisibility dropped over me, and it felt I was living on a different planet from my classmates. When *Game of Thrones* came out, I became an expert in the mythology of ice and fire. Then I got into *Skyrim* and *World of Warcraft* and all that. No one bullied you in fantasy worlds.

Once the outburst of violence stopped, I saw Will gaping at me with wild, puzzled eyes.

"She asked for it," I explained.

He looked shocked, speechless.

"Don't just sit there!" I yelled. "Take the fucking cart, and let's go. It's dog eat dog out here, man. Survival of the fattest!"

Will was too shaken to laugh at my joke. He did as I

ordered and took one of the carts. I pushed the other one and looked back to see if anyone witnessed my crime. No one did, or even if they did, they didn't care enough to do anything. Everyone focused on their own survival.

Will and I took all the canned food and water to the kitchen and then went into the living room. We had five jugs of water. At fifteen liters each, it was enough to last us two weeks.

We decided to barricade the house. First, we locked the porch and the front door and set a small couch from the living room against it. We agreed to only use the side door. We moved plywood from the basement to the garage, where Will cut it to fit the length of the bay window. At Will's request, I dragged the zombie's corpse out of our front yard and set it against a tree further down the street. Then I helped Will board up the bay window.

We noticed our neighbor Randy and his son did the same. Randy was a middle-aged man with a prosthetic leg. His son, Bobby, was athletic and wearing his Oilers cap backward. I hated Bobby from the start, your run-of-the-mill jock whose virginal mind never produced an original or creative idea. He never fought any real adversity. My judgment was reinforced by the Monster Energy logo tattooed on his neck. His idea of fun was probably getting high and blasting Pantera while cruising in his truck up and down Whyte, hunting chicks. Like Will and I, Randy and his meathead son were probably watching the game and having a few cold ones when the devastating news hit. Will went to talk to Randy, and I stayed behind. They agreed it would take time for the army to organize a rescue mission. Will recounted how I killed the first zombie and described the bedlam at Safeway—omitting our deadly encounter with Becky and her husband.

Randy's house was more exposed as he had no fence. Our fence wasn't much of an obstacle and needed to be reinforced. Other than Randy and us fortifying our homes, the rest of the street was infused in its usual sedated gray silence. Many residents had probably turned while at home and didn't have the basic knowledge to open their doors; left to wander around inside their places like doped rats in a maze.

Will finished visiting with Randy, and we went back inside. Exhausted, we plopped on the couches in the living room. It was totally dark, the only light coming from the flat TV screen that was now crawling with static. All my muscles burned and ached after the adrenaline rush. Princess came in and curled up at Will's legs. I lit up a smoke and took a long drag, my brain racing through the wild events of the last few hours.

"We should do something about that fence. Maybe reinforce it with some spikes and barbed wire," I said, though I had no clue where to get barbed wire from.

Will lit up a smoke and nodded thoughtfully.

After a few moments of silence, I said, "Hey Will, you know now that Becky and her husband are dead. Their place is basically ours."

"Uh-huh," Will managed. He looked like a puppet with its strings cut off.

"Anyway," I said. "I'm beat. I'm gonna take a nap." I climbed the stairs huffing and puffing. I didn't consider taking a shower and collapsed on the bed in my bedroom. Sometime during the night, I woke up from a hot, wet dream and popped a Prozac. I had forgotten to take it during the day. A thought cut through me, as cold and merciless as a scalpel. *I'm low meds, and the Safeway pharmacy is probably devastated.* A frigid chill went up my spine and froze my mind in the grip of terror. I had to talk to Will the next day about meds.

I figured Will, with his shuffling gait and skeletal appearance, could easily pass for a zombie. The following day, I gave him a red GoodLife Fitness duffle bag a tenant left behind and showed him a green and white Prozac capsule. His main goal was to find my meds, but he could bag whatever goodies he got his hands on. He returned with a few cartons of Pall Malls from 7-Eleven and a fifteen pack of Black Ice from Liquor Depot.

However, he said Safeway swarmed with zombies, and checking out the pharmacy was too risky. I believed him. The news hit me hard, though. I knew withdrawal from Prozac and didn't want to go through that shit again. Will said Becky might have some at her house. We went and checked. She had other kinds of meds, and I didn't know if they worked for me. Instead, we found two bottles of Jack Daniels and a Stalinskaya.

By the time we came back, there was no electricity. I went to my room and jacked off savagely over my favorite porn on my laptop before the battery ran out. Back downstairs, Will was hammered. We decided to make another run to Becky's house.

Luckily, we found a bunch of camping gear—Coleman gas lanterns, a portable stove, thermoses—which we carried back to our place through the back alley. Will decided we needed to cook the meat, so it didn't spoil. It must have been all the death surrounding us, that sense of reality itself brimming with malice, that made Will and I surrender to a strong Bacchic impulse. We ate and drank a few days in a row with complete abandon, from sunrise to sundown. In my hazy journey between blackouts, I puked in my room, on the stairs, and in the blooming bushes by the side door. The only positive thing we managed during that turbulent time was to put some buckets in the backyard to catch rainwater. It rained one day. At least we were good for water.

One morning, I noticed with horror we were down to three cans of Black Ice and were choked by panic. My brain got zapped, and my vision blurred. I sat down on a chair in the kitchen, held tight to the edges of the table, expecting to be rocked by a full-blown panic attack. Nothing happened, but I was tense, feeling like a frog electrocuted by a decrepit Dr. Frankenstein. You never knew when the next jolt was coming, and it usually melted your body into pure anxiety. I waited a bit more, breathed deeply, and felt my muscles relax.

I descended a few stairs in the basement and called Will. Princess barked, but I didn't hear Will's grumpy voice telling her to shut up. I banged on his bedroom door. Still no response. I opened the door, and Princess ran out and up the stairs and sat by the side door, a sign she needed to go out.

Ashy sunlight filtered between the slabs protecting the small bedroom window, enough to make out the inside of Will's squalid room. On the right, there was a desk with an old, dusty desktop computer on it, an open jar of peanut butter, and a half-full bag of sliced bread sitting next to the keyboard. A decrepit small couch, Princess's bed, sat against the wall, the stuffing coming out of the pillows. On the left, there was a case of tools with a driller and claw hammer on top. Will still slept on the mattress on the bare cement floor. At the head of the mattress, a chair's seat served as the pharmacy, home of about a dozen brown prescription bottles.

The acrid aroma of excrement filled my nostrils. Princess took a shit on the floor at the bottom of the bed, which meant she had tried to wake Will up during the night but couldn't. A bit more concerning was the one-liter plastic bottle filled with murky urine sitting by the edge of the bed.

Will was snoring. I moved toward the bed and shook his shoulder. "Will, wake up, man!"

He opened his eyes, bathed in confusion. "Where am I?" he mumbled.

"You're at home, man. We're almost out of booze."

"Oh," he said, still uncertain.

I pushed, "Do you want me to make you some coffee, and then you can hit the liqueur store again?"

"Yeah, but later, Jeremy. I need to sleep more. I'm exhausted."

"Okay, man," I said. "I'll take Princess out and will come to check on you later. She left a stinky gift for you too. At least it's solid."

Will groaned.

I put Princess on the leash and took her out to do her business in the backyard. I lit a smoke and inhaled deeply, trying to calm my nerves. I knew I couldn't wait after Will. My anxiety would go through the roof. I needed to go to the liquor store myself, no way around it.

Back inside, I filled up Princess's dry food bowl and water, and then I put my hoodie on, grabbed my gun, and put on a comfy pair of Sketchers athletic shoes. I fetched the duffel bag Will had used the last time and, after a pause, I went outside.

I smelled the reek of putrefaction emanating from the hoard of the undead orbiting the Safeway. The block looked forsaken. I wasn't sure how many neighbors were still around but cleaning their front yards wasn't their priority. The melted snow uncovered half-buried cans, coffee cups, muddy bottles, deflated tennis balls from the nearby court, crumpled bags tangled in brown bushes. Wild green grass spurted from the cracks in the sidewalk and dotted the lawns, set to thrive in the powerful sun and the absence of cutters.

At the corner, fat crows pecked at the scattered skeletal remains of Becky and her husband. The killing seemed to have happened ages ago. From there, I saw the zombies. They looked like drunken fans at the end of a metal festival, still under the spell of the sinister music. I walked straight ahead toward 109th, the tennis court on my left. The large thick bushes in front of the chain-link fence of the court provided a good hiding spot for the undead—empty, battered sleeping bags of homeless people were visible through the greenery. Maybe one of the bums had turned and was starving for flesh.

I veered toward the outside edge of the sidewalk, counting on my peripheral vision to signal a zombie attack. I kept my head down and said to myself I was invisible. At the corner, I gazed to the left on 109th. The road was blocked by a pile-up of damaged cars and a fire truck resting on its side— an annihilated prehistoric beast. Someone drove their blue Toyota through the front windows of the Garneau Pub, dislodging the pool table. In the distance, through the morning haze, the Edmonton skyline appeared like a foreign, distant citadel, given the almost complete paralysis of transportation. Groups of the undead roamed through the quiet desolation like gloomy survivors of a war-ravaged area.

Walking briskly, I crossed the street and turned right. The liqueur store was at the intersection of 109th and Whyte. I reached the corner and looked down Whyte. It, too, was jammed by damaged or abandoned cars. The Pawn Shop, the closest nightclub across the avenue, was charred, a decayed tooth among mostly unblemished structures. The front windows of the two banks next to it were broken. A group of zombies banged against the doors of the O'Byrne's Pub, a block away on my side.

I pushed open the door to the liqueur store. My heart sunk. In the murky light, it looked like all shelves were empty. However, as my vision adjusted to the gloom, I spotted a few lonely bottles—also, the two aisles on the right might hide some elixir. I decided to first check the cooler at the back, where they kept the big cases of beer. I opened the door and saw a dark figure crouched down in the corner. My blood turned to ice. It was a live guy with a hoodie like mine filling up his backpack with cans of beer. He felt my presence, looked back, and stood up quickly. It was a Native kid, my age, bigger than me. He looked as scared as I was. Quickly, he took a knife out of his pocket and flicked it open. "Get the fuck away, white boy, this is our store. Or you want to get scalped?"

For a moment, I froze. No one had threatened to cut me up before. But then my survival instinct kicked in. I pulled the gun from my pocket and squeezed the trigger. The bullet punched a hole in his face, blood and brain matter splattering the wall behind him. He slumped to the floor.

The gunshot would attract zombies. As fast as I could, I fit two fifteen packs of Black Ice into my duffle bag. Then I dragged the body through the cooler's door and left it at the end of the first aisle. Panting already, I ran to the last aisle away from the entrance and grabbed a few bottles of hard liquor at random. I heard the door open—the store filled with the smell of decay and the sound of hungry moans. I almost retched when the stench of rotten eggs and excrement hit my nostrils. The door closed behind two cadavers. I fetched a bottle and threw it against the cooler's glass, right where the Native guy lay dead.

The moans became high-pitched, and soon I heard the wet, smacking sounds of the undead gorging on my victim. I grabbed my bag and went to the door. Already, two pairs of necrotic hands tried to push it open. Running out of time, I got a good hold of the bag and tucked it close to my body, opened the door, and rammed through the undead like a football running back. The fetid stench of rotted meat brought tears to my eyes. I hit the one on the right in his chest, and it went sprawling on the ground. The one on the left tried to grab me, but he was too slow. The flailing skin of his fingers rendered them useless. On 109th, groups of zombies shuffled

STILLBORN GALLERY

toward the commotion but there was enough room for me to run around them.

Back home, I collapsed on the floor, trying to catch my breath, my heart fluttering. "Three more days of life," I shouted with joy. Princess ran to see if I was okay and if I brought any treats. I petted her, and she wagged her tail. "Three more days of life, you fat stupid dog!" *Don't call her that. You're gonna give her a complex,* I heard Will scolding me in my mind.

I picked myself off the floor, set the treasure on the table, opened a bottle of vodka, and gulped it like water. Soon, the alcohol hit my blood, and a pleasant warmth engulfed me. After a few more drinks, I was perfectly numb, everything was far away and insignificant, nothing could pierce my cozy bubble. I didn't know what day it was and didn't care. I could still recall my own name, though it seemed like useless information.

I took the bottle and my faithful handgun, went upstairs, and read and drew. Unfortunately, I had no music. After a while, I felt the need to masturbate. I searched desperately around the room but found no material. I was hoping for at least a magazine with a hot calls section. I hadn't gotten lucky in like two years, and it got to the point I thought of fucking my linty belly button just to remember how it felt.

This made me chuckle as it reminded me of Gwen, my friend with benefits from high school, this dirty-minded chubby girl. One day she let me fuck her belly. She just squeezed my penis with her stomach fat, like I was fucking her tits. It worked pretty well. I came a healthy, thick jet. Then Gwen, before eating the cum like a good sport, started doing these masticating movements with her cellulitic stomach as if her belly button was chewing gum. Gwen was amazing—too bad she moved to BC. Those sex images were too faded in my mind to provide any real stimulation, though.

I had a few smoke breaks and took Princess out. The neighborhood was quiet and desolate. I went down to the basement a few times, and I could hear Will's snores through the door. Except now, he also groaned while sleeping as if in physical pain or the grips of a nightmare. Soon after the light bled out of the day, I passed out as well.

Next morning, I had cereal for breakfast and boosted my coffee with a big splash of whisky. Tipsy and energized, I grabbed my handgun and banged on Will's door. When no reply came, I opened the door all the way for light to come in. The smell was fouler than the day before. I sat down on the mattress and shook Will's bony shoulder, not even sure if he was alive. He turned slowly on his back and looked at me with dazed, watery eyes.

I said, "Will, it's me, man. You've been sleeping for days."

"Jeremy," he managed with a weak and raspy voice. "I'm not feeling well." His black mouth produced a fetid odor that almost made me gag.

"Really, cause you look peachy," I joked, and Will tried to laugh but ended up coughing dryly. There was a rusty secretion around his lips that didn't look like saliva.

"Based on the smell, it looks like you shit yourself, Willyboy. You literally shit the bed."

"I know...fuck." Will attempted to laugh again and then coughed. Some of the droplets hit my face, and, on closer examination, turned out to be blood.

I put my left hand on his chest. Under the clammy skin and protruding bones, I could feel his galloping heartbeat and a deep vibration as if his lungs were boiling. I asked in a grave voice, "Will, you're in pain, man?"

He squeezed his eyes shut, tears streaming from the corners down into the grimy pillow.

"No more painkillers, morphine, or anything?"

His eyes still shut, he shook his head.

"Will, I can make the pain go away, man." He opened his eyes slightly, saw my gun, and I could feel his frail heart beating faster. But he didn't struggle. "There's no point suffering like this, my friend."

He grabbed my left arm with his bony hand and looked straight at me. "But what if the army comes?"

I looked down and shook my head, "No, man, I talked to Randy yesterday, and he said they'll only come in winter when all zombies are frozen. It's easier for them to clean everything up in winter."

"Oh," Will sighed, deflated by the lie. Then he squeezed my forearm and looked at me intensely. "But what if I go to hell? Suicides go to hell, Becky said."

I bit my tongue and struggled to stay calm. This act of mercy killing turned out to be more difficult than expected. I felt like I was building a ladder for Will, a fake ladder toward nowhere. But I needed to make it sound like the phony ladder was going somewhere. It was like being a midwife but only in reverse, stuffing a bag of bones back into the vaginal canal of the abyss.

"No, Will," I said. "I'd be the one killing you, no suicide. And you're already in hell, man, constant pain, no hope, squalor, what can be worse than this?" I gestured vaguely around the room.

Will looked around the desolate room and nodded.

"Plus, God will take mercy on you, man. You've suffered so much. What's Jesus' cheap stunt on the cross compared to your years of battling cancer and heart disease?"

He squeezed his eyes and began crying again. A cockroach scurried across his forehead, but he didn't notice.

"Don't worry, my friend," I said in a soothing voice. "I'll take good care of Princess. She's in good hands. We'll find a way to get out of this mess."

He squeezed my hand again and nodded. "I hear you, son. I trust you."

"Hey Will," I said joyfully, "do you remember that day after a storm when Princess found a tree branch on the sidewalk and tried getting it through the door, but it was too long, and in the end, she figured out she had to go sideways with it?"

A smile pulled at Will's cracked lips, and he looked past my shoulder toward the ceiling, his eyes filled with the happy memory. I squeezed the trigger, and the bullet punched his head and bloodied the pillow. His hand gave me one more squeeze and then went limp. Princess came in and stood by her master's head.

☣

Waking up from a wet dream involving Gwen, my erection pressed against my crusty underwear. I masturbated on a towel almost stiff with filth and hardened cum. Then I threw it on the grimy gray carpet, next to dried-up chunks of vomit. The sun blazed in the room, dust particles dancing in the light. Layers of dust covered my desk and bookshelves, but cleaning appeared like a distant possibility. It would be a long summer day, but the usual things that happened during summers were conspicuously absent: no student parties, no nightlife, no festivals, no groups of girls sunbathing in parks, no nothing. Just eerie silence and desolation. This summer was like the scenic decoration of a postponed play.

I was sweaty, and my linens were shiny and faded from filth. I got out of bed and applied moisturizer in between my upper inner thighs as they'd gotten chaffed from rubbing against each other. My gray underwear was ripped, stained, and odorous. I rubbed moisturizer over my junk, too, aiming to keep it clean. Then I sprayed Febreze in a wide arc around the room. Pleased, I descended the stairs in the kitchen and prepared a coffee spiked with a shot of whiskey.

Princess came upstairs, and I checked her snout and teeth to see if she started chewing on her master's bones yet. I haven't seen any skin or traces of rusty blood, so I gave her some dry food.

Once I finished my boozy coffee, I decided to scavenge Becky's house again, in case we missed anything. I inserted the handle of the claw hammer through one of the belt loops of my shorts and placed my gun in my pocket. Out in the back alley, I saw a lone zombie stumbling down toward me, coming from the direction of Becky's place. At first, it looked like a drunken woman. Then I saw the gash wound on her neck, her dislocated jaw and vacant, milky eyes behind a curtain of greasy black hair. She wore a black shirt saying *Love Pink* in sparkly print. Her tight blue jeans were soiled with excrement, and she was missing one of her sandals.

Under the flimsy shirt, I could see the straps of her bra and the contours of large breasts. My penis responded instantly to her cleavage, and I grabbed my claw hammer. When she got close to me, she growled and lurched. I pushed her hands aside and buried the metal claws in her temple. As soon as she went down and stopped moaning, I kneeled by her body and ripped her shirt and bra. Pierced nipples topped her livid, wrinkled breasts. Above the left tit, a calligraphic tattoo read *Girlicious 69*. In the same style, the ink above the right one advised, *Carpe Diem!* A white cesarean scar ran down from her navel.

I squeezed her breasts and sucked on them with thirst. I soon got fully hard, pulled my shorts down, and stroked myself, gently rubbing her purple nipples against the tip of my cock. Her frozen, mangled face kept distracting me. I half-expected her busted jaw to move and speak in a gravelly voice, *I have no gag reflex, hun. Blow and go forty dollars. Best headgame on the Southside. No teeth.* While her crooked mouth vomited this ad, I imagined her eyes would stay vacant, the top half of her face petrified. Only the muscles of her jaw would briefly spring to life following a random neural flare. I took off my t-shirt and covered the freakish visage.

I gazed around. There was no one in sight, alive or dead. I focused on those large, sagging breasts, twisting and pulling and rubbing them, trying to ignore the acrid smell of feces and decomposition wafting from the body. Soon I came, two thick jets flew out in succession like two phlegm-wads glistening in the sunlight—the first one on the asphalt and the second one in the cleft between her breasts.

I pulled up my pants and stayed there on my knees, huffing and puffing. I grabbed the t-shirt covering her face and put it back on, blood and drool cold on my skin. I examined her head and was overwhelmed by a desire to break her skull and see her brain. I pulled the hammer out of her skull. It made a wet sucking sound. I used the claws to cleave her head around the nose line and break it in half like a coconut. The brain appeared gray, soft, semiliquid, like a rotten fish in a clamshell. Maggots infested its ridges and crevices. The sewage stench made me tear up. It was a wonder the zombie could even walk. Its two eyes dropped in the neural muck like two boiled eggs in a clogged toilet.

Absentmindedly, I spread the rancid brains on the gritty asphalt with the head of the hammer. I scrambled the bits of maggoty neural tissue with the glop of sperm. A bit of random info came to mind: sperm is alive up to five days after ejaculation. I thought, *Wasn't sperm some sort of vital energy? Weren't neurotransmitters like serotonin the agents of life in the brain?* Suppose I placed the mixture of seed and infested brains back in the skull and glued the cranial bones back together and shook the head like a bratty kid does a broken toy. Would Girlicious 69 come back to life like a Franken-

STILLBORN GALLERY

hooker? The thought made me chuckle. My seed was as wasted as a serotonin molecule adrift in the post-synaptic cleft.

Even with the head now pulverized, the body was still good, especially the torso. I poured the fetid gelatinous stew with eyeballs on the ground and hid the corpse in our garage for later use. I knew a dead body decomposed slower in a closed space. I noticed a handsaw on the workbench that would allow me to cut her disgusting head off later on. Out of the garage, I took one last look down the alley. Plump crows already gathered around the grayish muck of brains and semen splashed on the ground, one of them closing its beak around an eyeball and flying up in a tree.

I craved a drink and made my way down the cement pathway along the backyard. A dark thought hit me like an ax: I was a sperm cell convulsing in a wad of ejaculate melting in the sun, on a forgotten alley in a dead town. I was just that, frantically struggling in vain, engaged in a chaotic battle inside a plasmatic abyss, the expiry date looming large on the horizon.

ZAP!

My brain flipped, and my vision clouded. The electric shock went from the top of my head to the tips of my fingers. The jolt depleted all my energy reserves. My bones were too heavy for my flesh, my flesh too heavy for my will. I felt I had a ball and chains attached to my legs and each step became small and laborious. The house seemed far away as if seen through the wrong end of binoculars. It moved farther and farther with each heavy step I took. The cement of the pathway turned to quicksand, and I was slowly sinking.

I meant to scream for Randy, our neighbor, but my mouth and vocal cords were nothing but dust. I tried to grab onto Randy's fence boards. My hands were waxy and lifeless. Our backyard looked far away; the crab apple tree, the buckets for collecting rainwater, the unused barbecue, the plastic table, and chairs, all seemed as remote as moonscapes. The flutter and calls of sparrows hidden in the tree's foliage were cast-iron weights of loneliness and abandonment.

I'm being buried alive in this shallow grave, and nobody knows, I thought bitterly. *Nobody cares. My parents don't care. Will is dead. But why should anyone care for a wad of phlegm on a forgotten alley in a dead town?* That venomous thought led to full paralysis as the cement swallowed me whole. I succumbed to the tightening darkness. Except there was no "I" anymore? "I" was an evaporating dream. What remained was a trembling point of fear and disgust, a black hole of naked anguish. What happened was the unholy funeral of Mr. Nothing.

Part of my frenzied mind knew I had collapsed on the sidewalk in some kind of catatonic fit, like a mechanical toy that ran out of batteries. I don't know how long I laid there, but I remember lighting up a smoke. This simple process took forever as my hands seemed the hands of a puppet on strings I was just getting a handle on. I grabbed my pack from the right pocket and emptied it on the ground as picking a smoke directly from the pack required too much coordination, and I was nearly blind. I managed to stick the cigarette in my mouth, hoping it was with the filter first. I inspected with my dry tongue, and it felt like the filter. Then I fished my lighter from the left pocket and flicked the wheel. After a few sparks, I managed to get a steady flame and take the first blessed deep puff.

Then I raised my right hand, palms up, and I stabbed the cigarette on the pale, tender inside of my forearm. A jolt of pain shot up my arm as the smell of burnt flesh invaded my nostrils. I clenched my teeth and my eyes teared up. The minor burn situated and focused me. I repeated the gesture till I felt in complete control of my body again, Jeremy the Hero struggling to survive the zombie apocalypse.

Dizzy and nauseated, I stood up slowly and made my way to the house on rubbery legs. Inside, I drank half a bottle of vodka like water and then managed to stumble up to my room and pass out on the bed.

I woke covered in a film of sweat as the late afternoon sun blistered through my window. I was surprised to see I had a raging hard-on again. Armed with my bottles of Febreze and Vaseline and my switchblade in my pocket, I made my way to the garage to visit my new girlfriend. I opened the door and blasted the air freshener in the direction of the body to cover the smell of corruption. As I stepped into the dim-lighted garage, I saw two fat rats scurrying to the dark corners. I seemed to have interrupted their snacking on Girlicious' toes as three of them were missing.

Her head looked like a rotten cantaloupe cut in half, adorned with a black wig and a pair of dentures. I got the handsaw from the workbench, grabbed her neck with my left, and cut with my right. It got more strenuous when I got to the spinal cord, my forearm aching from the effort, and the self-inflicted cigarette burns.

As I got closer to finishing the cut, the head shook from side to side as if to negate further desecration of her body. But it was too late. She was but a filthy human condom. I tossed the abused head into a dark corner, dinner for the rats. Black blood oozed from her neck like sludge from a sewer pipe. Around that discharge, the cross-section looked like a dried-up hamburger. I fetched my knife and carved a bigger hole around the esophagus opening. Then I lubricated it with moisturizer. The makeshift vagina wasn't very enticing, and my dick seemed to shrivel up.

I closed my eyes and started stroking myself.

I'm in a back alley by Whyte, and I see Girlicious 69 rushing toward one of the nightclubs, doing her power-walk in her high-heels like an authentic discount Beyoncé. *I come out of the shadows and ask, "How much for a bj?" She looks at me like I'm a cockroach in her cereal. "You could never afford me, you fat slob," she spits. I stick my gun in her face, and her eyes go wide. "Then you'll have to blow me for free; you used human condom!" I point with the gun. "Get in there by the other dumpster and get down on your knees!" She does what I say, and a motion-sensor light comes on, illuminating the scene. I follow her. "Good, now show me your tits!" She takes her top off and reveals her goodies, and I proceed to slap them with my right as I hold the gun with my left. Soon they turn red, and she's crying. "Open your trap, whore!" She obeys and I shove the barrel of the gun down her throat, pressing against her teeth. "Fuck, what's with those teeth? Was your father a donkey?" I ask and laugh heartily. Then I smack her head with the gun. She falls on her back. I press my boot on her throat, harder and harder, till her face turns red and then blue. I squash her like a bug.*

Fueled by my imagination, my full erection throbbed. I pushed myself into the corpse's neck. If reaching third base felt like warm apple pie, this felt like cold beef jerky. While not impenetrable, the neck was very resistant. Soon, I settled into a rhythm, imagined eroticism pushing away the squalor of reality, and, after a sweaty grind, I managed to come. It felt painful and awkward as if something blocked the full release of sperm. When I pulled out, I noticed my dick was smeared with cum and moisturizer. Something move. My breath caught in my throat. As small as bits of rice, a few maggots slithered from under a few drops of cum and crawled into my penis opening.

My heart sunk. I gave a high-pitched girly scream. I walked outside with my penis in my hand, wiped the discharge off it, and looked at my open palm closely in the bright light of the sun. I couldn't see any movement. Was it possible some worms crawled up her esophagus from her infested stomach and then leached onto my cock? Maybe they burrowed inside the flesh with their tiny hooks, and some of them were ejected by the jets of semen? That would explain the sense of blockage that disturbed my climax?

Should I shoot my dick off? Burn it? Cut it off?

My head spun, my cock got smaller and smaller, my jaw clenched. "Fuck," I shouted and punched the outside wall of the garage till my knuckles turned red. This was too much for me to bear in only one day. With shaking hands, I gathered the Febreze, the moisturizer, and my knife, and went back inside the house.

I drank heavily to bury the more distressing aspects of the day and muster some positive thoughts. I told myself my eyes played a trick on me in the murky light of the garage. Maybe my tormented brain produced a hallucination. Wasn't most of perception a fabrication of our minds, anyway? I played fetch and tug-of-war with Princess till I felt like hitting the can. It burnt to urinate, and my piss had a rusty color. I quickly flushed the toilet. I made a mental note to maybe take a shower the day after.

☣

Later that night, I took Princess out and lit up a smoke. The heavy silence was only disturbed by crickets singing in the high-grass and the buzzing of mosquitoes. Through a gap in the fence, I saw Randy's large basement window. He hadn't boarded it up, probably relying on the dense bushes flanking it. From where I stood though, I had a perfect view inside. In the yellow glow of candles and gas lamps, I could see a mirror on top of a dresser. A naked woman came into view—a beautiful, live woman walking around nonchalantly.

I choked on my smoke as my heart pounded against my chest. I must have looked like a sailor spotting a mermaid on a crop of rocks, pipe falling from his mouth. The angelic apparition was short and slender, with a perfect hourglass figure. She had a firm, round ass that begged to be spanked. Her long brunette, wavy hair draped over her shoulders to the tops of her apple-shaped breasts—no sag there, just perky, jiggling beauty. She swayed her wide hips as she walked back and forth to the dresser on lean, tout legs. She brushed her hair and spoke to someone out of the line of vision.

Something wet touched my hand. I looked down and saw it was a rope of drool. I sucked some of it back while the rest fell on my t-shirt and the ground.

"Argh, any port in a storm, lad," a voice said. "You came a long way, seaman."

It was Will's voice. I looked at his boarded-up basement window, half-expecting his head to pop up, a skeleton grin on his face.

"Fuck, I thought you were busy decomposing," I said. Princess cocked her head, curious how come I was talking to Will when her master was not in sight. "And that's not any port in a storm, you idiot, that's top-quality solid meat right there."

"This being dead thing made me crave a smoke," Will said, and then it sounded like he pressed on a lighter. "She's a nice piece of tail. You're right on that score." Will continued, exhaling the smoke. "Did you see her pubic hair is shaped like a heart?" Sounds of lips smacking. "Better than that ugly thing you got in the garage there, you sick puppy." Raspy laughter followed by coughing.

"Wait, you knew about this hottie, and you never told me?" I asked, still looking at Randy's basement transfixed, waiting for another appearance.

"Yeah, I see her almost every night since I suffer from insomnia. But there's not much you can do about it, spud. She's with Bobby, Randy's son. And he's built like a house of bricks. When's the last time you hit the gym, eh?" A dry, spluttering chuckle.

Now it was my turn to take a deep drag. Eyes squinting, wheels already turning in my head.

"Oh, I see what you're doing," Will said in a raspy voice. "You're itching to get yourself killed over a piece of tail."

"She's not just a piece of tail," I said through clenched teeth. "She's water. And I can't survive without water."

Will had no answer to that.

I took Princess inside, rushed upstairs, and wanked savagely in the darkness. It hurt and burned when I came. It felt like I had barbed wire stuck in there. I laid in bed thinking for a long time, twisting and turning in the filthy sheets. My angel was right there, twenty feet away from me. My life would be so much better once I had her, a live sex slave. That was the serotonin boost necessary to go on. It was the fountain of holy water I needed to rejuvenate and regain my vigor. I couldn't sleep until my plan was set in detail and my mind made. And that was when the first pale rays of sunlight leaked into the room.

When we fetched it from Becky's place, the gas lamp came with a red gas canister. I placed the canister by the front corner of Randy's house and then took Princess for a morning walk. The horde of the undead outside Safeway thinned to about fifty. We got closer to the pitiful procession, and I urged Princess to bark. "Get them, Princess, you savage dog! Rip those freaks to pieces, you fearless beast!"

The first sharp barks cut through the mortuary moaning, and some undead heads snapped in our direction. What looked like a nightmarish Special Olympics race started toward us. A woman in a wheelchair had the lead. Its muscle memory must have been good as its fat arms pushed the wheels with mechanical precision. Its head and upper body leaned forward, eager and predatory. It had a round baby face and frazzled white hair. The knife plunged in its right eye covered half its face in gore. Its mouth was already making chewing motions, and a rope of saliva dripped on its palsied legs. Under the remnants of an Edmonton Eskimo t-shirt, its massive wrinkled boobs pressed on its skinny knees.

To the woman's left, I recognized one of the hippies in our area. Its body was tilted to the right, its long dreads mopping the gore and filth from the pavement. Some of the undead held things that were in their grip before they turned. I knew that even after a traumatic head injury, the brain could recall some routine activities. A mother pushed its squirming undead kid in a stroller. Some zombies pushed carts, carried bags or baskets, or car keys. An old couple still walked together, bodies joined like Siamese twins, their mangled, desolate faces looking in opposite directions.

I've watched the freak show transfixed as Princess continued barking beside me, in full attack mode, jumping up and down in a frenzy. When I deemed the zombies close enough, I pulled on Princess's leash, and we ran back to the house. I let her inside and then ran back to the front of Randy's place. I fetched the canister and threw gas on the front of the house as high as I could, making sure to cover the window boards as well. The gasoline sparked in my nostrils as I jerked the can back and forth, defacing the house with a golden shower. I tossed the empty canister aside, fetched my lighter, and ignited the accelerant. A grin spread over my face as the flames shot out and up, peeling off the paint, turning the wood from white to brown. Then I took a lap around the house through the back and to the other front corner. I crouched down, waiting for the rats to come out, my gun at the ready.

As the fire engulfed the outside wall, the zombies came into view, the wheelchair monstrosity still in the lead.

Sure enough, after a few minutes, I heard the door being unlocked and the screen door banged open. Randy and his son came out swearing. Randy carried a fire extinguisher.

Bobby, his Oilers cap turned backward, brandished a machete. Randy sprayed the foam over the fire as Bobby moved to face the zombie procession. Excited by the sudden commotion, the paraplegic corpse moved faster; its wheelchair smacked the curb and catapulted it onto the ground. Unperturbed, the zombie used its massive arms to crawl through the weeds, sensing the fresh meal.

Bobby approached the corpse and decapitated it in one swift motion. The head rolled in the grass, mouth making chewing motions, knife still stuck in its eye-socket. As Bobby turned to kill the next zombie, I fixed my aim on his large back, inhaled deeply, and exhaled through pursed lips. I squeezed the trigger. The bullet plunged into his back. The jock managed to turn toward me and charge wild-eyed, his machete slicing through the air. I shot again, and his ball cap flew up as the bullet pulverized his face.

I turned to Randy, my weaker opponent. He looked like a deer in the headlights, the fire extinguisher in his limp hand. I put two bullets in his chest before his brain had a chance to compute the gruesome developments. He fell with his back against the remaining flames and uttered a few piercing screams. Desperately, he crawled toward the zombies, his back on fire, the sharp odor of burnt meat infusing the air. Drooling zombies tore at their morning barbecue. The horde was too close, moaning feverishly, crowding the front lawn. I turned and ran into the house and shut the screen door and the door behind me. I locked it with trembling fingers. I turned around a triumphant smirk on my face.

"He came with a machete to a gunfight," I murmured.

"You shot Bobby in the back like a coward," Will said.

"I just outsmarted them, that's all. Natural selection at work, old man. Survival of the fattest. And now time for reproduction," I said and giggled.

Will kept quiet.

I began looking for my prey. I found her sitting on a bed, in a bedroom on the main floor, holding her knees against her chest. Under her tight black skirt, I saw her pink panties. They matched her Hello Kitty short socks. My dick throbbed to life. I needed to be cool and execute the final step of the plan.

"Zombies are coming!" I shouted. "We have to run through the back door before they surround the house." I pointed with my gun in the direction of the kitchen door.

"Where's Bobby?" she asked in a small voice.

"They got him, unfortunately. He's one of them now. Come on, we're running out of time." I put my gun in my waistband and extended my left hand to her. Reflexively, she grabbed it, got her feet on the floor, and stood.

I knocked her out with my right fist, not hard enough to kill her, just to render her unconscious. Then I lifted her over my shoulder. She was tiny but still pretty heavy. The feel of the smooth back of her thighs made my cock leap up hungrily. I opened the back door, ran through Randy's backyard, and made my way past bushes and through the broken fence between the properties. I glimpsed to the right. The horde pressed on the outside wall of Randy's house, some catching fire like torches. I frantically opened the side door and, in my rush, I hit my prize's head on the wooden frame. Muscles burning and knees feeling weak, I dumped her on the floor and locked the door. I collapsed and took a breather. The hardest part was behind me. Now it was time for the sweetest part.

I dragged her into the living room by her arms. The Coleman lantern radiated an incandescent white that mixed with the pale light from the hallway. My victim still seemed to be out of it as I peeled off her skirt and panties and ripped off her top. Enchanted by the naked, live body, I took my shirt off and pulled down my pants.

I sucked on the pink and smooth nipples of her perky tits. Then I filled my mouth with their freshness and bit on them. I watched with fascination how my bite marks turned red with her bright blood. It meant she was warm and alive, as opposed to my frigid ex. As my mouth released a thick rope of saliva, I went down on her. I closed my eyes and inhaled deeply the sharp, earthy aroma of her genitals. I fingered her pussy and flicked her clit gently with my tongue. To my surprise, I've heard her moan and thought I maybe had a nympho on my hands. Encouraged, I inserted two fingers into her wet warmth as I lapped at her clit like a thirsty dog. Then I sat up and began stroking myself before penetration. In addition to the throbbing pain of my erection, I felt something wet and gelatinous down there. I looked down and screamed.

ZAP!

The brain jolt amplified my impotence. My vision blurred as I saw my tormented cock puking thick globs of a yellowish substance streaked with blood. My dick was the angry red of a purulent zit, and its discharge crawled with fat maggots.

I jumped up on my feet, grabbed the gun, and pointed it at my damaged penis. I screamed again and squeezed my eyes shut. I could feel the barbed wire twisting again in there, except now it was burning hot. Viscous blood leaked down my leg.

I pressed the trigger.

The loud bang and gruesome sight paralyzed and catapulted me into a dark protective space. I was petrified. A wave of shock pulverized most of my consciousness. As if walking on stilts, I staggered toward the couch and plopped down, eyes staring at the bedroom as if through a long black tunnel, slowly turning into a statue of fear.

Princess walked into the room and lapped at the wormy muck on the floor. But I was so high on anxiety I couldn't care less. I moved my eyeballs slowly toward my groin. Blood spilled from a hole in my upper thigh. *I failed again*, I thought, a hot tear dribbling on my frozen face. *I'm such a useless abomination I'd botch my own suicide. I'm but a half-dead exhibit in a freak show. Unfit for life and unfit for death.*

The dark carousel of morbid thoughts made any sort of movement seemed physically and intellectually impossible. Was my brain supposed to send a signal to my arm's muscles? Who sent an impulse to the brain? No one has shown me how to send anything to my brain. I must have missed that class. How strong should the impulse be? What if it's a weak one and only travels halfway to the muscle and then fizzles out? Mobility was paradoxical and absurd.

Attracted by my screams and the gun blast, the zombies began banging and scratching at the boarded window behind me. The noise seemed far away and insignificant, but I couldn't help but be awed by their single-minded determination, their exuberant vitality, their unquestioning fervor. The zombies were the new apex predators, the top of the food chain. They were light-years ahead of me on the evolutionary scale, as I was a concentrated point of fear, a particle of anguish, regressing to the cold silence of the mineral realm.

ABOUT AXL BARNES

Axl Barnes is a horror writer and philosopher from Edmonton, Canada. His novella *Ich Will* and first novel *Odin Rising* are available on Amazon in Kindle and Paperback. He's currently working on his second novel, *This Town Must Burn*, and several sick and twisted short stories.

For more information and free content visit:

axlbarnes.blogspot.com

twitter.com/axlbarnes
instagram.com/axl_barnes

ABOUT THOMAS STETSON

Having had (has) aspirations in the medical illustration field, Stetson utilizes his subjects to describe a mental collapse and a personal apocalypse.

He has a dozen or so self-published zines through the pseudo company, Foul Apparatus. Now almost entirely focused on larger single pieces.

He currently resides on the outskirts of humanity in northern Vermont.

Artus Collective:
https://artuscollective.org/thomas-stetson/
Facebook:
https://www.facebook.com/foulapparatus

Made in the USA
Monee, IL
27 April 2021